WHEN MY TEARS CRY

By

Vanessa Hollis

Published by Teardrops Publishing
& Vanessa Hollis
ISBN 0-9767602-1-5

Additional copies of this book are available by mail
Send $17.99 each (includes shipping and handling) to:
318 Gentry's Walk
Atlanta, GA 30341

Or pay through PayPal on my website @
www.teardropspublishing.com
www.vanessahollis.com
& through Amazon.Com

Printed in the United States by Morris Publishing
3212 East Highway 30
Kearney, NE 68847
1-800-650-7888

TEARDROPS PUBLISHING

ACKNOWLEDGEMENTS

I first would like to thank my maker, for without him in my life this wouldn't be possible.

I would like to secondly thank my mother Margaret (Pudden) Rowland who is and forever will be the love of my life. It was brought to my attention that I failed to mention her contribution of giving me the name of the hotel near the hospital. Okay mom, here's your spot. I would like to thank my silent financial supporters, you know who you are. And to my little sister Terri Rowland, for her continued contribution of poems that she manages to be on point with each and every time. All I had to do is ask and she delivered. And my book club back home in Tulsa, Essence thanks for everything.

To everyone who had a technical hand in this book, I would like to thank you for all of your experience and patience. And my girl Joyce Hunt of Mitchie's Gallery in Austin, TX...who gave me that chance...many, many thanks.

My continued thanks to my son Termaine Yargee, who has not only been in my corner from beginning to end, but who has managed to reach his peer group and encourage them to support my efforts. Much love to you from mom. And to my granddaughter Mekyla Yargee, who puts a big smile on my face, just in thought about her. Love always Bink Bink.

This comes from your mom, your sister, your daughter and your friend. Vanessa 06'

CHAPTER ONE
THE PENDING QUESTION

As Mekyla watched the bags on the baggage carousel she felt Ian put a hand on her back, gently and tentatively.

"We have a lot to talk about Mekyla," he said.

Mekyla sighed. "I really appreciate you coming to pick me up Ian. I do. But I can't talk about my feelings right now. I need to see how my sister is doing." She spotted her bag on the carousel and pointed to it. "There's mine. Would you grab it for me?"

Ian leaned over the carousel; arm outstretched and waited a couple of seconds for the bag to get to him. He let the handle come into his hand and snatched the bag up. "I'm talking about after you see Christy." They turned and began making their way through the crowd of people still waiting for their luggage. When they'd cleared the thick of the crowd, Ian put the bag on its wheels and pulled out the handle. He looked around to make sure they were out of earshot of everyone. "But I do need to know if you slept with him." he said.

Mekyla raised an eyebrow at him. "No," she said emphatically and started moving again. "I didn't sleep with Jonathan. I didn't even talk with him the whole time I was there."

"But you wanted to, right?"

"Ian, please. Can we discuss this after?"

They made their way to the truck in silence. Mekyla slipped into thoughts of her sister. She just wanted to get to the hospital and see her family. She needed to assure herself that Christy was all right.

Ian tossed the bag into the trunk of the SUV, then unlocked the passenger door and held it open for Mekyla. He made his way around to the driver side and climbed in. "Do you really expect me to just stand by like a good boy knowing you went off to Texas chasing after another man?" He started the truck and backed out of the space.

"I knew this was a bad idea," said Mekyla. "I should have followed my first mind." She put her hand up to her head and rested her elbow on the car door panel near the window. "You know Ian, you're making it very hard for me to want to come to the house with you later."

"I don't know if I even want you to come to the house." Ian's voice was low and brooding.

"Fine."

"Yeah, fine. I guess you think I'm some kind of punk or something. I try to hold your hand at the airport and you pull away. I put my hand on your back and I feel you flinch. I hold the truck door open for you and you don't even say 'thanks.' I don't know what I'm doing in this relationship."

"Ian, would you rather I call one of my sisters to come and pick me up?"

Ian glanced over. "Pick you up from where, the highway?" His voice was raised now, angry or maybe just indignant. "Mekyla, would you just sit back and relax. I said I would take you to the hospital, so that's what I'm going to do. I keep my word."

Mekyla turned and stared out the window, hiding her face from Ian. Her eyes were stinging and when she blinked, tears rolled down her cheeks.

"Did you want to go straight to the hospital or would you like to stop by the house to shower and change?" Ian's voice had mellowed.

Mekyla cleared her throat and tried to keep her voice from cracking as she spoke. "No, if you would just take me directly to the hospital I would appreciate it." She leaned the right side of her head on the headrest.

"Are you hungry?"

"Yes, just a little bit. I only had a bag of expensive potato chips on the flight home."

"I'll just drop you off at the hospital, then bring you something back."

"Thank you Ian." She sniffled once and not wanting Ian to start asking if she was all right, she found something to keep her busy. She dug into her purse and came up with her cell phone. "I should call Schonda to find out what floor Christy is on." Covering her face with her phone hand, she wiped the tears from her cheeks with the other.

She composed herself as the phone rang.

"Hello?" said her sister's voice.

"Hello Schonda, this is Mekyla. What's up?" She was

happy Schonda sounded composed.

"Hey Mekyla, this is Tere. Schonda is getting settled into a room."

Mekyla slumped down in the car seat. "What? A room in the hospital? She's having the baby?"

"Yes, she's in labor and I thought you wouldn't make it in time. Are you close?"

"What, you wanted to deliver my niece or nephew, huh? Sorry little sis, but yeah, I'm here. Ian's driving me to the hospital right now. We're just a few minutes away."

"That's good. I know Schonda's going to be happy to see you."

"So how is Christy?"

"I haven't been back up to see her, but she came through what she was admitted for okay."

Mekyla gazed out the window and rolled her eyes at her little sister. "Either you went to school on the short bus, or there's something more to what they found wrong with Christy. And from the way you're talking in codes I guess I'll just wait until I get there to find out what it is you're not volunteering."

Tere gave a short, tired chuckle. "Mekyla, it's good to hear your voice. Hurry up and get here."

"What floor are you guys on?"

"Oh. Christy's on the twelfth floor and Schonda's on the ninth."

"All right. See you in a little bit. Bye."

Mekyla folded her phone and tucked it back into her purse. She could feel Ian looking at her. After connecting with Tere and the status of the family, she felt more grounded. But she still wasn't ready to get into it with Ian and she hoped he wasn't about to start up again.

"So, did I hear you correctly? Schonda is also in the hospital?"

Good, she thought. Just concentrate on the family. "Yes, she's in labor. Everything's happening at once. Tere was pretty vague concerning Christy. I'm a little worried."

Ian turned the car into the hospital driveway. "Okay, we're here. I'm going to drop you at the door and then run and get you something to eat. What floor should I meet you on?"

"I'm going to check in on Schonda first thing to see how far along she is. But by the time you get back, I'll probably be with Christy. That's the twelfth floor." She stuffed her purse into her carry-on bag, then opened the door.

Ian patted Mekyla's knee. "All right. See you in a little bit."

Mekyla tried to force a smile as she got out.

As Ian pulled away, Mekyla stood for a moment staring up at hospital in which she and every one of her sisters had been born. "Hello St. John Hospital. The last time I was here was when my granddaughter was born. Now I'm here to see two of my sisters. This is going to be a long night."

CHAPTER TWO
GIVE ME THAT STRENGTH

Mekyla heard her phone ringing and dug it out of her purse. "Hello?"

"Hey mom."

"Hello Termaine."

"Are you in town?"

"Yes, I just made it to the hospital. Where are you?"

"Oh, I'm turning a few corners. I was there earlier. I had to bring Auntie Schonda's kids up there."

"Have you had a chance to see my granddaughter?"

"Well, her mom and I are still trying to work things out."

"I know its going to happen for you Termaine. Just keep your eye on the prize."

"I know. Am I going to see you tomorrow?"

"You always know how to get a hold of me. Call me tomorrow and maybe we can grab lunch."

"Sounds good."

"Well, I'm getting ready to get on the elevator, so I'll talk with you tomorrow. Love ya."

"Love you too mom. Glad to know you're back home safe."

"Thanks baby, goodbye."

"Bye."

Mekyla got off the elevator on the ninth floor and went directly to the nurses' station. She waited for the nurse to get off the phone so she could ask for Schonda's room number, but before she got the chance she heard a familiar voice calling to her from down the hall.

"Mekyla! We're over here," said Tere.

Mekyla hurried down the hall toward her sister. "Hey you. It's really good to see you."

"How was your flight?"

"It was fine. You won't believe it, but I was sitting next to a woman who asked if she could read some of my manuscript. And guess what she does for a living?"

"What?"

"She's a publisher."

Tere gasped and swatted her big sister's shoulder. "Get out. So, is she going to be the one to put you on the shelves?"

"I don't know. It's still too soon to tell. But, that's enough about me for the time being. Where's Schonda?"

Tere turned and started to lead the way. "She's down this way. You look like you lost some weight."

"I think I lost about five pounds or so. I didn't really eat right while I was in Austin."

"And this guy you went there to see, how was that?"

"It's a long story. Tell you about it later." Mekyla said, as she followed Tere into Schonda's room.

Schonda looked up from her bed and smiled.

"Hey Schonda. So you thought you'd have this kid while I was in Austin." She set down her overnight bag and approached the bed.

"Mekyla. Glad you could make it. I'm glad I didn't have to choose between Tere and Kimberly, because that was going to get ugly."

Mekyla stood by the bed and took Schonda's hand. "How are you feeling?"

"A little anxious, but that's to be expected."

Mekyla nodded. "I remember the feeling. How close are the contractions?"

"They're about forty-five minutes apart."

"Where's Deon?"

"He's around here somewhere."

"So does this mean he overrides me?"

"Yes and no. He said it was okay for you to help with the delivery, that he'll just sit back and watch."

"Oh, how noble is that! So where are mom and Kimberly?"

"Mom's upstairs in Christy's room and Kimberly is

somewhere trying to find something to snack on."

"Yeah. Christy. Well guys, on that note, I'm gonna head up to see my girl. I'll be back down later, okay?" She picked up her bag again and headed out the door.

"Hold on Mekyla," said Tere, coming up behind her. "I'll walk with you to the elevators. Christy really won't talk to any of us. Maybe – well, I know she'll talk to you. So if you would, just let us know if there's anything we can do to help her out. I don't even know if Trey ever showed up to see how she was doing."

Mekyla pressed the button for the elevator. "I'll talk to her and I'll listen. I guess that's really all I can do."

"I don't know what's going on," said Tere. "I don't know whether I should be upset with him or not. But we do know that there's something else wrong in addition to why she's here in the first place. She just doesn't want to say."

The elevator doors opened. Mekyla stepped inside and turned to face her sister. "I'll try and find out. I'll see you guys later," she said as the doors closed.

Mekyla drummed her fingers nervously on the counter at the nurses' station until a nurse was free to speak with her.

"Hello, I'm Christy Love's sister – another one. Could you direct me to her room?"

"Sure, just one moment." The nurse consulted a sheet of paper then looked up and pointed. "Her room would be down this way and it's the third one on the right."

"Thank you very much."

Mekyla entered Christy's room quietly and immediately saw that both her sister and her mom were fast asleep, Christy in her bed and their mom in the reclining chair next to her. She eased her bag down to the floor then leaned over to give her mom a kiss on the cheek. Her mom opened her eyes with a big smile on her face.

Mekyla whispered, "If you keep that snoring up, you're going to wake up the whole floor."

"Hey baby," said her mom, her voice a little raspy with sleep and perhaps worry. "When did you get in?"

"Just a little while ago. I stopped by to see Schonda first. So, how is Christy doing?"

"Oh I guess she's doing just fine. The doctor said that this may have disturbed her other situation."

Mekyla sighed and looked down at her sleeping sister.

"And what are these situations?"

"Well I know what the initial reason is for her being in the hospital, but we don't know what the other situation is. She won't talk to me and the doctor wouldn't say."

"Has Trey been here?"

"I haven't seen him. Maybe he hasn't checked his messages yet."

"Mom, you think you can give me a little time with Christy?"

"Sure baby. I'm glad your back home. And I know Ian is glad as well. You really shouldn't leave your man for long periods of time like that. They do have needs, you know."

Mekyla scowled a little at the thought of Ian. "Yeah, okay mom. I'll be down in a little bit." She helped her mom up out of the chair.

"It's a good thing you showed up. I believe Kimberly and Tere would have fought for your spot in helping Schonda deliver her child."

"I heard. Mom, have you been dreaming about fish lately?"

"No. Why do you ask, are you pregnant?"

"I was just curious. I was thinking about how you would always know when one of your daughters was pregnant. Because you started dreaming about fish." Mekyla heard footsteps outside the door and turned to see Ian entering the room.

Ian gave a half wave to Mekyla and then smiled at her mom. "Hello Mrs. Brinkley."

"Well, hello Ian. I was just talking about you. You're looking well."

"Thank you ma'am."

"Oh, you don't have to call me ma'am. You know you can call me mom." She gestured toward to white paper bag Ian was carrying. "What you got there?"

Ian lifted the bag. "I brought Mekyla back something to eat."

"Oh and what did you bring her?"

"I went by the Chinese restaurant to pick her up some shrimp fried rice, since I knew that was her favorite Chinese dish."

"Ooh, that sounds good. You know I started taking my girls to that restaurant there on Yale about twenty years ago. Is that the place you got this from?"

"Yes ma'am."

"Mom, would you like to have some?" said Mekyla. "I'm sure there's plenty."

"Nah baby, you go ahead and eat. If there's some left over just bring it down to me. I'll go down and sit with your sister for a little bit." She started to leave the room.

"Mama?" said Mekyla.

Mekyla's mother stopped and turned. "Yeah baby?"

Mekyla furrowed her brows and smiled. "Did you know that your shoes didn't match?"

"My socks don't match neither."

Mekyla tried not to laugh. "Okay. Well, I guess you were in a hurry to get here, huh?"

"Mrs. Brinkley," said Ian. "It was good seeing you."

"It's good seeing you as well, Ian. Well, I'm going to head back down to sit with Schonda. Don't be a stranger Ian, even though my daughter is."

Ian chuckled. "I won't."

Mrs. Brinkley walked out of the room and Ian turned to Mekyla and lifted the bag again. "I'ma put this over here on the table and I want you to call me when you're ready for me to pick you up."

"It's probably going to be very late Ian. I have to help with the delivery of Schonda's baby."

Ian nodded. "Just call me. When you're ready – whenever it is – I'll come pick you up. It doesn't matter if I'm at work or not, just call me."

"I will. Thanks Ian," Mekyla said, as she walked Ian to the door.

He paused in the doorway. "You know, even though we're going through what we're going through, that doesn't change the way I feel about you. I'm still very much in love with you. You're going to have a baby." He placed his hands on Mekyla's shoulder and he looked her straight in the eyes.

"Okay, I'll call you later," said Mekyla, hoping Ian didn't hear the uncertainty in her voice.

Mekyla stood by Christy's bed for a moment. Her sister was down for the count. They must have given her some powerful sleeping pills. Part of her wanted to wake Christy up so that they could talk, because at some point, she'd have to go into the delivery room with Schonda. But she knew the best thing to do right now was to let Christy sleep. Then Mekyla began thinking about the off limits room with the graham crackers Jennifer raved about when she spent so much time visiting her grandmother. Then again, she had the Chinese food Ian had brought. But with all the stress of having two sisters in the hospital, she seemed to have lost her appetite. She nestled herself into the hospital recliner chair from hell, picked up the remote, and turned on the TV with the volume turned very low. She flipped through the channels, hovering for a moment on HBO, but that was just some B action flick and Mekyla wasn't in the mood. She found Lifetime. Lifetime channel is always good, she thought. Now, with nothing more to do than wait, she suddenly felt how tired she really was.

CHAPTER THREE
A SISTER'S LOVE

Tere stood beside Schonda's bed and looked down at her with a look of exhaustion. "Do we have to stay here now that Mekyla's here?"

Schonda scowled at her sister. "Yes, you have to stay here."

"Why? We're not going to get to cut the cord or do anything."

"Because you're my sisters and I need your support. And besides, Christy is still here as well. You have two sisters here who need your selfish support."

"Oh, I know. I'm just getting tired of eating these graham crackers that Kimberly swore were so good. I think I'ma go out and get something to eat."

"Like what, Tere?"

"I was thinking about some fish." She smiled and gazed out across the room. "Yeah, some blackened fish from the Black Eye Pea Restaurant."

"Ooh," said Schonda. "That does sound good."

"What sounds good?" Mrs. Brinkley said as she walked into the room carrying the extra blanket from Christy's room.

"Mama, we were just talking about going out to get something to eat," said Tere. "I thought about some blackened fish from the Black Eye Pea."

Mrs. Brinkley chuckled. "That's funny. Mekyla was just asking me about fish, but yes, bring me some back."

"Me too," said Schonda, turning away from the monitor that helped her to recognize when she was getting ready to have a contraction. "I'll have whatever you guys are having."

"Schonda," scolded Mrs. Brinkley. "You know you can't have anything to eat other than ice."

"How do they expect for me to just stop eating when I'm now accustomed to eating at least six times a day?" said Schonda in a slow, sad voice. "Besides, it's not fair for all of you to eat and not me. Mama, I'm hungry."

"I know baby. I'll give you some of me and Mekyla's Chinese food whenever she brings me my portion."

"That's a shame," said Tere as she walked around the bed to get her purse off the chair. "Hey Kimberly, are you going to ride with me?"

Kimberly thought about it for half a second. "Yeah, if you would swing me by Kentucky Fried Chicken."

Tere laughed. "I bet you go out of your way to find a Kentucky Fried Chicken when you're out of town on vacation."

"You know Tere, the only reason I do that is to see if they're uniformed. I'm even the same way with the Wal-Mart's. I always stop at a Wal-Mart in another city or state to see if they're set up the same way. And in some of my journeys I've found that some cities still don't have the Super Wal-Mart, what is up with that?"

Tere rolled her eyes and shook her head at Schonda as she turned Kimberly around by putting her hands on her shoulders. "We'll be back." She steered Kimberly out the door. "You're a strange bird Kimberly," she said.

They nearly ran smack into Deon as they left the room.

"Hey what's up Deon? Where have you been?" said Tere.

"I found some little packages of graham crackers in the staff only closet?"

"Poor thing, we're going out to get something to eat. Would you like for us to bring you something back?"

Deon's eyes lit up as he reached into his pocket. "Yes. Here's ten dollars. Just bring me what you guys are having."

"I'm having fish from the Black Eye Pea, and Kimberly's having Kentucky Fried Chicken."

Deon rubbed his hands together. "Ooh, that sounds

good."

"What, the fish?"

"No, I want the chicken. The two piece all white with some mash potatoes and corn on the cob."

Tere smirked. "Whatever. Kimberly, grab your chicken partner's money and let's go."

Kimberly took the ten dollar bill from Deon and started down the hall with Tere. "You know, not everybody eats at restaurants on a daily basis like you and Ashton. This is a treat for some of us and we just want what we want, that's all."

"You guys can afford it if you didn't spend your money on a lot of other things."

Kimberly looked at her sister. "Yeah, like what, utilities and rent?"

"Maybe if you find yourself a husband or man, Kimberly, maybe he'll take you out on a regular basis, instead of waiting on special occasions like Valentines Day. But first you have to pick the right one, and none of the ones you already have will do."

They stepped onto the elevator and Kimberly pushed the button for the ground floor. "Maybe I like the fixer-uppers."

"No, I think you settle for the fixer-uppers."

"Let's not start, Tere. Just because you've found yourself a nice man with a degree and goals, don't hate on me."

"Kimberly, you have a degree."

The elevator doors opened and the two sisters strolled across the hospital's lobby and out the front doors.

"For some reason the educated men I run into are always stuck up," said Kimberly.

"*You're* stuck up."

"All the more reason for me not to have a man that acts the same way I do." Kimberly shrugged her shoulders, as if the point she was making should have been obvious.

Tere laughed. "You are a piece of work Kimberly, a very interesting character."

The sisters got into Tere's car. "Why are you so broke anyway?" said Tere.

"By the time I finish making payments on my student loans, paying rent and everything else that comes with just being out on your on, I'm working to just live. I know our father said never settle for less. But let me tell you something sister, I will accept a hundred dollars a month from a man at this point."

Tere turned out of the hospital parking lot into traffic. She scowled at her sister. "Don't ever say that to anyone else, Kimberly."

CHAPTER FOUR
THE PAIN OF LOVE

Mekyla was just starting to get into the movie she'd found on Lifetime and the shrimp fried rice Ian had brought her when she heard movement in the bed. She turned to see Christy's eyes wide open, looking straight at her. Mekyla began to smile.

"Hey you," said Christy.

Mekyla stood up and set the Chinese food on the nightstand. "Hello sweetie. Boy, I see I can't leave you alone for a long period of time." She bent down and gave her closest sister a big bear hug. "How are you feeling?"

"I stay too sleepy to feel since I've been in here."

"So do you want to talk about what got you here?"

Christy sighed. "Yes and no. For the first time in my life that I can remember, to be truly scared to share with you what I have to share." She struggled up into a sitting position. "Because I know once I say it to you, it's going to make it surreal." Tears welled up in her eyes and she wiped them away with the backs of her fingers.

Mekyla sat on the edge of the bed and rubbed her sister's shoulder. "Christy, you just don't know how calm I've tried to remain. You really scared me and no one would tell me what was wrong with you, and trying to stay calm while in front the Kimberly, Tere, and Schonda was hard. Then there's mom, I didn't know how much longer I could keep up the façade."

Christy sniffled and managed to get herself under control. "A little over six months ago, I discovered I had breast cancer."

Mekyla looked at Christy for a few moments in a state of disbelief of what she'd just heard. Mekyla stood up and just continued looking into Christy's eyes. "No, no, please don't tell me that."

Christy wiped away a few more tears.

Mekyla took a deep breath. "Okay, so, it's in remission, right?"

Christy shook her head. "No, no it's not. I've tried to tell you about this so many times, but there was always something else going on in our lives."

"What something else? What could be more important than you sharing this with the family? You know I know what it is, you're always worried about everybody else that you never made time to care for Christy."

Christy shook her head, unable to speak for a moment.

"So this is the cause of you losing so much weight?" said Mekyla. "I thought it was the stress from your marriage."

"Well, I'm sure that played a role in it as well, along with the stress of knowing I had cancer."

"So if this is the thing that the rest of the family didn't know about, what actually caused you to have to come to the hospital that they know about?"

"A couple of days ago, I discovered . . . ."

Mekyla's cell phone rang and she grabbed it, thinking it might be someone calling from Schonda's room. She looked at the caller ID display. "Oh, it's Jennifer."

"Don't answer that call," said Christy.

"I wasn't," said Mekyla, with a look of confusion at Christy. "I was just putting it on vibrate. This is the third time she's called me. I'll call her back later tonight." She switched the phone to vibrate and held it in her left hand. "Please continue with what you were going to tell me."

"We were at home one evening and Trey was in the shower. His cell phone rang. Something it's been doing more frequently these days and at late hours. So this time, I answered it. And it was her."

"Her who, Christy?"

Christy pointed to Mekyla's cell phone.

"Somebody on the cell phone, I understand. But who was it?

"Jennifer."

Mekyla recoiled a bit. "Jennifer who?"

"Your friend Jennifer."

Mekyla tried to get her mind around what Christy was telling her, but she wasn't sure she was following it. "So, what did she say she wanted with Trey?"

"She said she was sorry I answered the phone, but she

guessed I would eventually know. I said, 'know what?' And she said that she would really rather tell me and Trey at the same time. Well since I wasn't really getting anywhere with that particular conversation, I was curious to know how she got Trey's cell phone number, so I asked her."

Mekyla sitting there holding onto every word that was being said. "And, what did she say?"

"She said that she had it for a long time. All I could think was, 'this cocky heifer.' And right then I knew that she was having an affair with my husband."

"An affair, Jennifer and Trey, no, they couldn't be. You really feel they're having an affair?"

"Yes. And that's not all of it."

In a low whisper, Mekyla replied, "There's more, of course there's more huh? You don't just end up in the hospital over some news, unless you're really old I guess, but please continue."

"While I'm talking to Jennifer on Trey's cell phone, he steps out of the shower, walks into the room and asks me who I'm talking to. I said it's Jennifer on *his* phone."

"He just stood there looking at the phone and I handed it to him."

"And what happened? What did they talk about?"

"After he says hello, I hear him say, 'What do you mean I have a son?' I turn to look at him. I said, 'What?' And he turns to me and says, 'She's claiming that her son is mine.'"

Mekyla shook her head. "Oh no, he couldn't be."

"I asked, 'what son?' But he turns away from me and starts trying to have a private conversation with Jennifer. So I get all up in his face and I start screaming my questions. Then he pushes me away and I bump my arm on the corner of the night stand. He hung up the phone, put clothes on and left the house. I haven't heard from or seen him since."

Mekyla put a hand on her forehead. "Okay, hold up," she said. "Are you saying to me that Jennifer is telling Trey that Junior is his son?"

Christy shrugged her shoulders. "Mekyla, I didn't even know Jennifer had a kid, let alone Trey's. And why didn't you ever share this with me?"

"I just found out myself. She shared it with me a few days ago, but she told me the father lived in Louisiana. Remember, she had to go on a trip to Louisiana?"

"I remember her going, but I never knew why?"

"She told me the father's name was – what did she say his name was? Hold on, it was a name I was familiar with. Oh I remember, it was Brent, I remembered saying that it was such a coincidence because I have a policyholder that moved in from Louisiana with the same name. And she made some remark like, 'all the men in Louisiana have good genes.' I never really understood why she said, 'all the men in Louisiana', as if she'd been with them all."

"I don't know anything about that," said Christy.

"So, they kept you in the hospital because of a bruise on your shoulder, or did you have some type of reaction because of the cancer?"

"No, it wasn't the bruise or the cancer that caused me to be checked into hospital. I took too many pills at one time."

Mekyla looked up at the ceiling and sighed. "Why would you – okay I know why. But, I mean, well, why would you do that to yourself Christy?"

Christy looked down at her hands in her lap. "I didn't want to live. At first I was very scared to go through with it. I laid all of the pills out on my vanity, looked at them literally for hours. And the whole time, of course, I was crying my eyes out, trying to unravel what went wrong, or when it went wrong. I thought back to when we were in college and that encounter we had at LSU's football game, and I remembered that I thought at that time she had a crush on Trey. But I just blew it off."

Mekyla took one of her sister's hands and held it in both of hers. "Christy, you do realize this is not your fault. I don't know if I can say it's Jennifer's fault either. Unless, your suspicions were correct that they're currently having an affair."

Christy pulled her hand away. "I know you're not taking her side?"

Mekyla gasped. "Of course not, it's just that this is too much for me to absorb right now. Besides, what I'm saying is that if the kid is Trey's, Jennifer had him before you guys were married. But of course, that doesn't address the issue of whether they're having an affair now."

"What I'm saying is that he's had a thing for her all these years, from then to now, and he married me anyway."

"This is just so much. And on top of all that you have cancer." Mekyla shook her head. "You have cancer, Christy.

I'm not going to lose you. I can't lose you Christy." She grabbed her sister and they hugged each other tight.

They held each other for a while. Each wiping away tears. Finally, Mekyla stood up straight and asked, "So, when do you get to blow this camp?"

"I guess whenever they decide that I'm no longer a danger to myself. But I honestly don't know if I'm ready to face these additional things that I have before me."

"I'll be right there with you, every step of the way."

"I appreciate you so very much Mekyla. I'm going to need you now more than ever."

Mekyla sat on the edge of the bed again and patted Christy's hand. "Christy, there are a couple of poems that I read, I can't remember the authors. There were only a few verses that I have remembered and tried to live by or shared with other people to live by. In other words, I may accidentally run them together or leave something out."

Christy smiled. "I'm listening Mekyla."

"Okay, the gist of it goes like this:

"Love begins with a smile, grows with a kiss and ends up with a tear. The brightest future will always be based on a forgotten past, so, you cannot go on well in life until you let go of your past failures and heartaches. May you have enough happiness to make you sweet, enough trials to make you strong, enough sorrow to keep you human, and enough hope to make you happy. Because, happiness lives for those who cry, for those who hurt, for those who have searched and those who tried. Dream what you want to dream, go where you want to go, be what you want to be, because you have only one life and one chance to do all the things you would like to do."

"That was beautiful," said Christy. "Thank you for that. You were done, right?"

Mekyla held up a finger. "I'm going to say this one more thing and then I'm done preaching. There was this passage in the bible, I don't remember under what verse, so I may be just paraphrasing. *'My grace is sufficient for thee, for my strength is made perfect in weakness.'* So Christy, whenever you feel you can't reach me in your mind, I want you to turn to the man above and ask for guidance. Because I truly believe and know that he would not put more on us than we can bear."

CHAPTER FIVE
THE STORY OF JONATHAN

There was a knock on the open door and Mekyla turned to see Kimberly and Tere stroll into the room.

"Hey Christy," said Kimberly. "Is Mekyla preaching to you?"

"So Christy, what did the couch doctor have to say about your situation? You know, about you playing with more than one pill at a time?"

"Forget you Kimberly. Besides I haven't seen that doctor yet. So, how is Schonda doing? How far apart are her contractions?"

"I think they're a little over or under and hour. I'm not real sure. Do you remember Tere?"

"I think they're a little under an hour apart."

"I guess I owe you guys an apology for scaring you the way I did. It's just that I have a lot on my plate right now. Stuff that Trey and I are going through."

Kimberly turned to Tere. "I told you Trey had something to do with this."

"Kimberly!" Tere said as she rolled her eyes.

"It's okay Tere, Kimberly was right. Where are my kids?"

"They're at Trey's parent's house," said Tere. "Because I knew mom was going to come up here to see you. Would you like for me to go by and pick them up when I leave here?"

"No, they're fine over there. Trey will pick them up, hopefully tonight, no later than tomorrow."

"Mekyla, when do you go back to work?" said Kimberly.

"I'm going back on Friday just to check in. I'm sure everything is fine. Marie is a very good worker and I have my colleague Taylor Ellis, stopping in every now and then."

"So that gives you one more day to rest before checking in," said Tere as she flopped across the foot of Christy's bed. "And then you'll have the weekend to really recuperate from your trip."

"I guess everything is going according to schedule as far as the baby coming," said Mekyla. "Now we prepare for their wedding. How is that coming along?" Mekyla said, as she picked up the carton of shrimp fried rice off the night stand to finish off the last of it.

"Mekyla, is that the Chinese food mama's waiting on?"

Mekyla froze with the fork half way to her mouth. "What do you mean, 'waiting on,' I didn't promise her that I would save. She said if there was some left over to bring it down. *'If,'* she said. I was hungry from the trip. I only had a bag of potato chips. Has she eaten?"

"Yes, me and Kimberly went out and grabbed some food a little while ago."

Mekyla let out a sigh of relief and kept eating her shrimp fried rice. "I'm really tired and I know that I'm going to have to show back up really early because Schonda is going to have this kid real soon. Excuse me while I step out to call Ian."

Mekyla took her cell phone and Chinese food and started for the door.

"So Mekyla," said Kimberly. "Are you cheating on Ian or what?"

Mekyla stopped in her tracks and turned around. "No, I'm not cheating on Ian. Well, not anymore. I guess you can say I got played by the person I was going to cheat with."

"Okay," said Kimberly, waving her big sister out of the room. "Go ahead and make your call and we'll come back to finish this conversation." She followed Mekyla into the hallway.

Mekyla looked at her with her jaw hanging down. "Kimberly, do you mind?"

Kimberly tossed her head back and walked back into the room as Ian answered the phone.

"Hello Ian, this is Mekyla. I'm ready whenever you can come pick me up. I'll be right where I was when you brought me the food. Or if you want you can just call me on my cell and I'll come down."

"I'll be there in just a little bit," said the voice on the phone.

Mekyla could hear an over-eagerness tone in his voice, like he was trying too hard to please. She wrapped the call up and rejoined her family in Christy's room.

"Okay," said Kimberly. "You know we've been waiting to hear the whole scoop on your trip for a while now."

"It's really nothing. A month ago, when I first went to Texas for the book convention, I met this guy at an art gallery called Mitchie's Gallery in town near where the convention was. If you're ever in town, it's a must stop by place. But heads up: I told Ian I met him at the convention."

"Ian knows?"

"Yes and no, but let me finish Tere. And the novel, has been changed to reflect some of our meetings in Austin, but enhanced a little of course."

"So your book is a romance story turned sour? Or did you have to rewrite the ending?"

"Yep, that's exactly what I did Kimberly, wrote myself right into denial."

"Oh, that's not true," said Christy. "This guy was crazy for her. He was driving all the way here to see you, right?" She gestured to her other sisters. "Tell them that story Mekyla. I think it's romantic." She adjusted her pillow to get a good view of her big sister as she told the story.

"Okay. Well, me and Jonathan hadn't talked or seen each other since my first visit to Austin. I had pretty much given up on what would have been. Then I get this wild hair up my butt to call him at his home. He answers the phone. I read this poem I had written for him."

Tere nodded enthusiastically. "You do write some beautiful poems, you and Schonda." She looked around the room for confirmation and everyone nodded.

"Thanks Tere. When I finished the poem he asked if he could call me back because his wife was there."

"Oh, yeah, I had forgotten about that part," Christy said, as she scrunched her shoulders up to her ears and grimaced. "But it gets better, right Mekyla?"

"Well, that was a low blow," said Kimberly. "How did you recover from that?"

"I recovered with a lot of water loss mixed with guilt. So, I returned to work on that Monday after the Sunday barbeque we had at Tere's house." She nodded toward Tere. "But when I got to the office, I found out that Jonathan had left a message on the answering machine there saying that his wife had only come by his place to sign their divorce papers."

"So, he *is* married?" said Tere.

"He *was* married."

"I thought we all vowed never to fool around with married men?"

"We did, and I'm sorry and paying for it."

Kimberly beaconed Mekyla with her right hand, "Please continue. I'm dying to hear this."

22

"Well, that wasn't all that was on the message. He also said that he would be driving in to see me that morning."

"Okay, now we're getting somewhere," said Kimberly.

"I waited and waited for him to walk through that door, but he never did. Then I started hearing from Christy and Marie about this accident that took place on Highway 75. Then I became anxious, almost frantic."

"I would be too," said Kimberly.

"Would you let her finish the story," Tere said, while looking over at Kimberly with a look of frustration.

"Well, you can imagine I couldn't work. So I go home and start trying to think of what to do next. Ian shows up and I'm just all over the place with craziness. I'm balling and Ian can't figure out what's wrong with me. So I tell him. I tell him about the trip."

"Oh, my, goodness," said Kimberly. "So what does Ian say?"

"Say about what?" said a voice from the door.

Everyone turned to see Ian entering the room.

"Ian," said Tere. "We were just asking Mekyla what you thought about her new bag."

"What new bag?" Ian said, with a look of confusion on his face.

"So, are you ready to go Ian?" said Mekyla.

Ian shook his head. "Yes, because I'm sure I'm not going to get any information out of the sisters. Here, let me take that bag." Ian took the bag from Mekyla and looked at it. "Looks like they're selling their brand new bags with the smudges and scuffs already on them, huh?" He smirked and turned to Christy. "Christy, how are feeling?"

"I'm fine Ian, thanks for asking."

Ian waved to everybody and back toward the door. "Mekyla, I'll be out in the hall when you're ready."

"Okay." Mekyla turned to see all her sister's looking at her. "Oh, shush. I don't want to hear it. Give me a kiss and I'll see you guys in a few hours I'm sure. Tell Schonda to hold off for at least four or five hours. I need the sleep." She kissed each of her sisters, Christy last of all. "I'll see you tomorrow Christy. Love you guys."

"Love you too Mekyla," said Tere. She leaned out the door. "Bye Ian," as she called down the hall.

She watched them walk away for a few seconds and

23

then hurried back into the room. "Okay," she said. "That was interesting, but how does it end Christy?"

"We all know that Mekyla took off for Dallas. This time she was going for closure."

"I thought it was Austin she went to?" said Tere.

"Originally, yes. But he was involved in that accident that she was talking about on Highway 75. The nearest hospital was in Dallas, so that's where they air lifted him to."

"Oh, okay," Tere said.

"She made it to Dallas, but when she walked into his hospital room she found his wife there."

Tere held up a hand. "Wait. You mean his *ex*-wife, right?"

Christy shrugged her shoulders. "Well, that's were I'm lost, because she never really got confirmation on the signature."

"Oh yeah," said, Kimberly. "That's right. Mekyla said that *he* said that she was there to sign the divorce papers."

Christy nodded.

"So, what happened next?" said Tere as she looked directly into Christy's mouth for answers. "What did she say she said?"

"I believe she said she just left and drove to Austin." Christy looked puzzled for a moment, and then her eyes lit up. "No, she said, her and the ex-wife spoke."

"Get out!" said Kimberly. "So, he's lying in his bed and Mekyla and the ex, or present wife are having words or Mekyla socked her in the face."

"No Kimberly, I don't think they had *words,* and no one socked anyone in the face. Well, not the way you're saying they had words, but they did have words of some sort."

Tere and Kimberly stared at her in anticipation.

"Oh," said Christy when she realized they were waiting on her. "But, unfortunately I don't know what those words were."

Tere threw up her hands again, exasperated.

Kimberly grabbed her cell phone. "I'm calling Mekyla."

"No you're not," said Christy. "What if Ian's around? She's not going to talk about it on the phone anyway." She lay back in the bed and folded her arm under her head.

"Those pills must have done something to your memory Christy."

A nurse poked her head into the room, and then came all the way in. "Excuse me, but the doctor is on his way in to see Mrs. Love. I'm sorry, but I'm going to have to ask you to leave for a little while, okay."

"Sure nurse," said Tere. "Christy, we're going to head down to see Schonda and then I'm headed home. I'll be back in the morning some time."

"Okay Tere. Love you, and drive safe."

"See you tomorrow sis," said Kimberly. "Love ya."

"Love you too. But, I guess mom will be hanging around all night, right?"

Tere rolled her eyes. "You know that lady ain't going anywhere until both of her daughters are out of here." She waved as she headed for the door. "Bye."

CHAPTER SIX
CHRISTY'S PROMISE

No sooner had Tere and Kimberly left, the doctor walked into the room. "Good evening Christy," he said.

"Hello Doc."

"How are you feeling?"

"Empty. I believe you guys fooled around and pumped out too much."

The doctor gave her a big grin. "At least we didn't pump out your sense of humor. That's good." He gestured to the woman standing to his left. "Christy, here's someone I would like for you to meet. This is Dr. Silloh. She will be visiting with you for the next couple of days."

"Hello Dr. Silloh, it's very nice to meet you. I'm really not a threat to my life. I was just going through something."

"And I believe you Christy," said Dr. Silloh. "It's just that I'm going to have to document it. I'll be back in the morning around 8:00 so we can go to my office and talk without any interruptions."

"Okay," said Christy with a shrug of her shoulders. "I'll be right here."

"See you Christy," said her attending doctor. "I'll probably be making one more round before leaving the hospital."

"Okay Doc."

CHAPTER NINE
DISTANCE

Ian tossed his keys on the kitchen counter. "Mekyla, you didn't say a word the whole trip home. Is everything okay?"

"I'm just tired, that's all."

"Are you hungry?" He hitched his thumb toward the refrigerator. "I can put you something together."

"No thanks. I'm just going to lay it down. You can have the bed. I'll sleep out here on the couch." Mekyla went and grabbed a pillow and blanket from the bedroom closet.

Ian leaned his back against the wall, crossed his arms across his chest and looked down. "And just how long is this going to go on Mekyla?"

Mekyla tossed the bedding on the couch and sighed. "Until we can both figure out where we stand in this relationship."

"You know where I stand and where I've always stood. I'm not the one that went gallivanting off to Texas to be with a lover."

"Please! Not now Ian. Can I just rest for a moment? All I want to do is rest." She flopped down on the couch.

Ian unfolded his arms and pushed himself off from the wall. "Mekyla, you know you can have the bed."

"I've already gotten comfortable on the couch, and I'm probably going to have to get up in a few hours to go back to the hospital to help Schonda deliver her baby."

"It doesn't have to be this way, you know. I'm angry, but not so angry to where I don't want you in the same bed as me."

Mekyla lifted her head, fluffed up her pillow and laid back down.

"I just want you to know that when you're ready to talk, I'm right here," said Ian. "Goodnight, Mekyla."

"Goodnight."

CHAPTER SEVEN
THE GUILTY CONSCIOUS

Jennifer pulled into her driveway, cut the engine and looked at her watch. She checked her cell phone to make sure it was on. "No messages, but it seemed to be working. Why hadn't Mekyla returned my call? For that matter, why wasn't anybody returning my calls. Something was wrong."

CHAPTER EIGHT
A MOTHER'S WORK IS NEVER DONE

Mrs. Brinkley put her hand on her daughter's face. "Schonda baby, are you sleeping?" she said.

With eyes closed Schonda nodded yes. "But it seems like every time I try and get some sleep a contraction starts."

"How close are they now?"

"They're about thirty minutes I guess." Schonda said, as she turned to try and get comfortable.

"Deon has taken the kids to the house to get some sleep. He didn't want to wake you."

"Okay. Why don't you just get in the bed with me?"

Her mother smirked. "There's not enough room on that bed for me and you Schonda. I'll call down and have them bring in a rollaway again. I had them do that when I was up in Christy's room."

"Mom you haven't even been home, have you? Better yet, why don't you go home for a little while?"

"I will when both of my daughters are leaving as well, not a moment sooner. The girls have brought me clothes to change into for the next day or so. And I've showered in Christy's bathroom and I'll use yours in the morning."

"If that's what you want to do mom, that's fine."

"In fact, you know what?" said Mrs. Brinkley. "I think I'm going to take that shower tonight. It may be chaotic in here in the morning." She turned and headed for the bathroom.

"Hey mom, why don't you call for the rollaway now, so it will be here when you come out of the shower?"

Mrs. Brinkley's eyes lit up. "Now that's a plan. That way I don't have to fuss with anything when I come out."

Tere got into bed and propped herself up with a couple of pillows. "Ashton, you will not believe all the stuff I've learned tonight, putting aside Christy being in the hospital, and now Schonda with the baby coming, listen to this. I've learned that Trey is having an affair or beating Christy and Mekyla was going to have an affair – well a cheating something or whatever."

Ashton aimed the remote at the TV, turned off the news and shook his head. "Hold on. Trey is having an affair?"

"Well Christy didn't really just come out and say that he was having an affair. But he hasn't even been up there to see her."

"Tere, that doesn't mean the he's having an affair. Maybe they had an argument or something."

"An argument and that would keep him from coming to see his wife when she's suddenly rushed to the hospital?"

"I'm not taking up for Trey or nothing, it's just that you've pulled a few little observations and comments out of the air and turned it into an affair."

"Okay, maybe I need some more information on that news item, but Mekyla is cheating, or did cheat on Ian."

Ashton chuckled and bowed his head. "See, here's the problem Tere. I know you're trying to get a reaction from me, but I also know that I'm doomed if I get involved and inquisitive and doomed if I don't respond. So, I'm just going to say this and let it go. Mekyla . . .," Then he threw up his hands. "No, you know what? I'm not even going to say that. I've listened to you baby, and now I'm going to sleep. Goodnight." He squirmed around adjusting himself to get comfortable in bed.

"Goodnight? But what about the part..., see this is why I don't share with you. You never get involved."

"Goodnight Tere," Ashton said, as he reached over to turn out the lamp.

Tere scoffed, exasperated. "Goodnight."

CHAPTER TEN
NIGHT VIGIL

Trey approached the nurses' station, looking up and down the halls trying to spot someone from Christy's family. Not seeing anyone, he leaned his forearms on the counter.

"Excuse me nurse. They told me downstairs at the information desk that my wife was on the twelfth floor, but I forgot the room number. Her name is Christy Love."

"Oh yes, your wife is two doors down on your right." The nurse said, pointing towards the room.

"Thank you very much." Trey flashed a smile as he backed away, finally turning in the direction of the room.

Trey slowly opened Christy's door, trying to be very quiet. He saw that she had her eyes closed and seemed to be sleeping, so he tiptoed to the recliner chair and sat down. He sat motionless for a moment, and then realized the remote for the TV was on the nightstand right next to him. He picked it up and took aim, figuring he'd spend some time watching the news and then head for home. He waited for the image to come up and made sure the volume was down low.

CHAPTER ELEVEN
THE SPOILED BRAT

Mekyla sat up straight, panicked by the sound of the phone. At first she wasn't sure where she was, but then she remembered she was on the couch and groped for the phone on the coffee table. While struggling to open her eyes, she noticed it was still dark outside.

"Hello?"

"Hello Mekyla, its mom. Schonda is very close in her contractions now. You probably want to come on down."

Mekyla cleared her throat. "I'll be right there mom." She hung up the phone and rolled off the couch onto her knees. That woke her up a little, but she was still stumbling and bleary-eyed as she made her way into the bedroom to find something to wear. She tried to be quiet, but she stumbled over a shoe and bumped against the dresser.

Ian jumped in bed. "What's the matter?"

"I'm sorry to wake you, Ian. I was trying to be quiet. I need to get some clothes out of the closet." Mekyla moved around the bedroom, using moonlight to see by so that she wouldn't have to disturb Ian any more than she already had. "It's Schonda. She's getting ready to have that brat kid of hers and I gotta go do my part."

"Oh, okay, do you need me to go with you?" Mumbling as he started to sit up in bed.

"No, go back to sleep. I know you're just as tired as I am."

He let himself fall back onto the pillow. "You can turn the light on if you like."

"I'll just grab my sweats. I'm sure this kid won't mind seeing Aunt Mekyla for the first time in sweats. Besides, the kid is going to have to get use to it. Because outside of the office, put me on a nice white tee shirt, a pair of jeans with some white socks, I'm in hog heaven, you know." She stepped into the sweats and pulled them up.

"I've always loved that about you, Mekyla."

Mekyla glanced over in the moonlight and smiled a curious smile. "What's that Ian?"

"You genuinely feel that you're simple looking. But I want you to know that I've always been crazy about you, whether you're in your power suit for work, or sweats, an old raggedy tee shirt and a pair of white socks. It never mattered to me what you had on. It was you I fell in love with."

Mekyla pulled a tee shirt over her head, and then paused for a moment, face to face in the semi-dark with something real about herself and her life. "Thank you for that Ian. I appreciate you more than I let on. But," she went on, her voice a little quieter now. "I don't think I have the heart to love you the way you want me to, or need me to right now."

"It's going to take time, and time is what we owe to that unborn child."

Mekyla sat on the floor with her back to the dresser and pulled on her socks and shoes. She didn't have the time or the heart to confront the idea at that moment. "I gotta go. Can we talk later?"

"Yes. We need to. Did you want me to buy take-out or would you like a home cooked meal?"

Mekyla chuckled softly. "I'd love a home cooked meal, but whose going to cook it?"

"That's very funny Mekyla, with your one dish, spaghetti special."

Mekyla finished tying her shoes and sprang up off the floor. "Gotta go, bye."

"Bye." Ian said. He crossed his hands and put them behind his head. He stared up at the ceiling and watched the moon shadows of the trees sway back and forth off the ceiling walls.

Schonda rolled her head back and forth on the pillow. "Where's my shot giver, mom? Why won't this kid get out of me? Didn't those people say that this will get easier the more you have?"

"Calm down Schonda," said Mrs. Brinkley. "I think they're referring to the number of children you actually deliver, and not the number of contractions you have during labor."

"Mama, I've been in labor now for eight hours, I'm tired and hungry."

"Nobody is more ready for my grandchild to come out than I am. Because until that happens, I can't go home and take these miss-matched shoes and socks off, since my daughters forgot to bring me another pair."

"Oh, no, here comes another one."

Mrs. Brinkley patiently patted Schonda's fist with her free hand. "Schonda, you're hurting my hand. Where is your sister at anyway? She should have been here by now. I wasn't a part of the who's-gonna–help-Schonda-deliver game."

Mekyla walked into the room ready for action. "I can hear you screaming all the way down the hall." She went to the other side of the bed and patted Schonda's forehead. "What's up little sis, are you in a little bit of pain? Do you need me to rescue you?"

"Mekyla, this isn't funny. Your job is to make these pains go away."

Mekyla pulled back a half step. "Then I volunteered for the wrong job. I just brought a pair of scissors from the house to cut the connection between you and my niece or nephew. End of job and I'm out."

"You're so crazy girl." Schonda said, as they all began to laugh.

"So mom, have you seen Christy this bright and very

early morning yet?"

"No. I was between both rooms up into the evening yesterday. I imagine Christy she should be sleeping very well now. But I haven't been up there since the girls left last night."

"How close are your contractions Schonda?"

"They're about two to three minutes apart."

"Okay, well let's get this kid out." Mekyla said, as she opened and closed the pair of sheers she brought from the house.

Schonda looked at her and raised an eyebrow. "Mekyla, you better go on with those scissors before you hurt someone. They have their own scissors here."

"Let's just use mine. I only paid maybe three dollars for them. If you use the hospitals it's going to cost you maybe three *thousand* dollars."

"Stop it Mekyla, you're making my stomach hurt."

Mrs. Brinkley stepped away from the bed for a moment to get a drink of water and Mekyla got a look at her shoes.

"Mama, for real. Are you really still walking around this hospital with two different kinds of tennis shoes on?"

"When I go home, I'm going home to stay. Both of my daughters will be fine and released from here."

"Let's wake everybody else up," said Mekyla. "Call Kimberly and Tere."

"They're not going to get up at four o'clock in the morning to come up here," said Schonda.

"Yeah they will." Mekyla held up the scissors, "*If* you lead them to believe that they're the cord cutter." She reached down and grabbed Schonda's hand.

"That's just wrong, Mekyla." Schonda's eyes closed tight. "Ooh, ooh."

"I don't remember that hurting that bad. Ouch, let go, let go of my hand. You're going to break it off. Mama, get her."

"Nope, I'm just an onlooker, just here to make sure everybody shows up for their positions."

"Where's Deon? I forfeit my spot. This girl is going to injure someone. They need to give you that saddle block shot, because the span of your hips apparently isn't blocking enough pain."

"What are you talking about, Mekyla?"

"Schonda don't know anything about the saddle block." Mrs. Brinkley looked down at Schonda. "Mekyla's talking about the epidural shot that they're going to give you if you decide not to have the child natural."

"Maybe we should call the nurse in, because they're getting closer."

"I'll go find her nurse," Mekyla said, as she began to head for the door but Schonda was still holding onto one of her hands.

"Oh no you won't, Ms. Coach," Said Schonda. "All we have to do is push that little button and they'll come down."

"Well they better hurry, mama. She's hurting me."

"I'ma call your sisters to come down," Mrs. Brinkley said. She grabbed her cell phone and dialed.

Tere answered on the seventh ring, obviously coming out of a sound sleep. "Hello."

"Hello Tere, its mom. Schonda's contractions are very close and Mekyla may not be able to stand the pain. Would you come down and take over?"

"She's not going to be able to stand the pain?" Tere groaned into the phone. "I told you Schonda should have picked me. Now look, Mekyla's going to chicken out and not even show up. I'm on my way," Tere said as she hung up the phone.

"Tere, I didn't – Tere? Oh, she hung up; she thought I said you weren't going to show up."

"Well, that's what you were supposed to make her think."

"Well I didn't want to lie to her though."

"You didn't tell a tale mom. I heard you. You said you didn't think I could stand the pain. That could have meant I was already here but was having second thoughts." She pointed to the phone in her mother's hand. "So, now do the same thing with Kimberly."

"Oh," Mrs. Brinkley said, as she began to dial Kimberly's home phone.

"Mom, I going to run up to see Christy real fast, just take hold of Schonda's hand, but be careful." Mekyla put Mrs. Brinkley's free hand in Schonda's.

"Wait, wait Meky . . . ." Mrs. Brinkley tried to pull away from Schonda as Kimberly answered the phone. "Hello Kimberly, this is mom. I need for you to head to the hospital. This girl is about to squeeze my hand off. Ouch! Ouch!"

"Mom, I'm on my way," said Kimberly.

33

CHAPTER TWELVE
THE BEAT OF MY HEART

Mekyla rounded the corner into Christy's room. "Knock, knock," she said, but she stopped short halfway to the bed. "Oh, she's not in here."

She started back to the nurses' station, but caught one of the nurses coming out of another room, just a couple of doors down. "Excuse me nurse. Where is my sister, Christy Love?"

"She's should be in her room."

Mekyla shook her head, her heart skipping a beat. "But she's not."

"Let me check."

"Thank you." Mekyla took a deep breath, trying to calm herself. When the nurse walked right past Christy's room, Mekyla stopped her. "Excuse me, this is my sister's room."

"Oh, I see where the confusion is." The nurse glanced back over her shoulder with a smile on her face. "We moved her last night to the room next door." She walked into the new room with Mekyla close behind. "Here we go," she whispered. "She seems to be sleeping pretty good right now. Maybe we shouldn't disturb her. Besides, her husband is here with her."

The nurse started to back out of the room, but Mekyla caught her by the arm. "Excuse me. Did you say her husband was here?"

"Yes." She stepped past the bathroom and looked into the corner of the room. "Well I thought he was still here. Maybe he went out another direction."

"Thank you nurse, I'll come back later. Better to let her sleep now." Mekyla said as she headed toward the elevators headed back to Schonda's room.

CHAPTER THIRTEEN
PAIN AND PANIC

"I'll be glad when Mekyla returns, because I can see you're getting ready to go into a panic looking at that monitor,"

34

said Mrs. Brinkley, still trying to pry Schonda's fingers open and get back her hand.

Mekyla heard her mother as she walked into Schonda's room. "Mama, why didn't you tell me they moved Christy?"

"Were you scared you wouldn't find your sister? That's what you get anyway for leaving me to do your job. Christy called down last night to Schonda's room and told us that she would be moving to room next door for whatever reasons."

"Well thanks for sharing, and that wasn't very funny. Now give me this maniac's hand."

Schonda took her eyes off the monitor to glare at her mother and sister. "Why are you guys talking about me like I'm not in the room?"

"Oh, everybody knows when you're in the room," said Mekyla. "Can't miss you babe."

"Just for that I'm going to squeeze your hand as hard as I can."

"I was just playing," said Mekyla, hurrying to try to calm her sister before she wound up with a handful of broken fingers. "You know you still look good to be as pregnant as you are. Anyway, I thought they were going to give you a shot or something?"

"They're on their way in to do that."

Tere hurried into the room in a near panic. "Mama, Christy is gone. She wasn't in her room and I couldn't find a nurse on the floor."

"Calm down Tere. They moved her to the room right next door."

"Somebody could have told me this before I. ..." She took a moment to gawk at Mekyla. "Why is Mekyla here? Why are you here Mekyla? Mama called me to come down because Schonda was close in contractions. She told me you wouldn't come."

"No, when she called I came right down," Mekyla said, as she put a puzzled look on her face.

"Oh, you need to stop it, Mekyla, said Mrs. Brinkley. "Tere, Mekyla had me call you and Kimberly to help her out."

Tere smirked at her sister. "You know that's wrong Mekyla."

"What, did we take you from your nice warm bed? Where do you need to be anyway? Ashton is the bread winner in your little family."

"That's right, I'm in school."

"You're always in school. How many degrees do you have now anyway?"

"I can't make up my mind on what I want to do."

"Good one," said Kimberly, strolling into the room. "Let's see how long Ashton, allows that to ride."

"Kimberly, what are you doing here?" Mekyla said, giving an award winning performance of being surprised.

"Mama said that you weren't going to show up, so she called me to come down. Tere, what are you doing here?"

"She called me as well. Actually Mekyla had mom call us both, just so she wouldn't have to be up by herself."

Kimberly looked down at Schonda and reached out to take her hand. "Hey Schonda, how are you doing, sweetie?"

"Uh-huh," said Mekyla.

"Ouch!" said Kimberly as Schonda tightened her vice-like grip. "Let go Schonda. What the heck. That hurts."

"Kimberly, now you see why I asked mama to call you guys, because this girl is crazy."

A nurse came into the room carrying a stainless steel tray with a needle on it. "Excuse me everyone. I'm going to have to ask you to leave for a little bit. We need to prep Ms. Brinkley her shot."

"We thank you very much," said Mekyla. "And our hands thank you very much."

The sisters and Mrs. Brinkley strolled down the hall into the waiting room. Mrs. Brinkley touched Mekyla's arm. "Did you find out what was wrong with Christy?"

"Yes, she's in here for taking too many pills."

"I know that much and I actually don't know why she did that. But what do you know about the other situation with Christy? The doctor wouldn't say."

"Actually mama, I don't feel comfortable saying either. Please allow Christy to tell you when she feels it's time."

"Okay, putting that to the side for now, did she tell you why she took so many pills?"

"Yes."

"And, what...?"

"Mama, you guys are really putting me in a bad spot. Didn't you sit with her for a while? Did she say why she wouldn't tell you?"

"She just said she wasn't ready."

Mekyla nodded. "Okay, can we please respect that and let it go for now?"

"I don't know why you girls are so secretive. This girl needs to go ahead and have this baby and Christy needs to be released, so that I can go to the house and get some rest. I'm getting hungry. Let's walk down to the cafeteria and grab something to eat."

"Mama, its five o'clock in the morning," said Tere. "And I don't know about that hospital food."

"Come on Ms. Sophisticated," Kimberly said, putting her arm around Tere's shoulder. "This food isn't going to kill you."

"I'm not hungry. I'll just wait here until the nurse leaves Schonda's room."

"All right Mekyla," said Mrs. Brinkley. "Would you like some coffee?"

"No, I'm fine, thank you mom."

"We're probably going to look in on Christy as well. So, we'll be back in about ten to fifteen minutes."

"Okay I'll be here." As Mekyla made her way back to Schonda's room. She poked her head in tentatively, watching for Schonda's reaction to the monitoring screen as her contractions came.

After a moment, she straightened up and went on into the room. "Oh good, I guess the shot took. You didn't scream to the top of your lungs when your contraction showed on the monitor."

Schonda smiled peacefully. "I'm fine. I feel good now. Come over and let me see you. I couldn't really appreciate your being here before, because I was in so much pain. You look well Mekyla. Tell me about your trip?"

"It was okay. Well better than okay. I did finish the book."

"Yes, the book. Tell me about it."

"I'd rather not. Not right now."

"Okay, not a problem. There's other stuff you could tell me, like how are you and Ian?"

"Another subject I'm not clear on right now."

"Are you guys in trouble? Is it because you were gone so long or had to leave for Austin again?"

"Yes and no. I met this guy when I went there the first time."

"You met a guy? As in, wanted to date him?"

"Yes."

"But Ian is such a good guy, why did you feel the need to look?"

"I don't know. It just kind of all happened fast. You know?"

"I was hearing some rumors from the sisters, but I just sort of ignored them."

"I think I'm just lost right now Schonda. I have so much on my plate."

"But is that a reason to cheat?"

Mekyla smirked at her younger sister's wisdom. "No it's not, but it's the only one I have right now."

"Find your focus Mekyla and dig deeper into your heart before letting something go again, to never get it back."

"Thank you for that. Here's my younger sister giving me good advice. Love you girl."

Schonda reached her hands out to give Mekyla a hug. "I love you to Mekyla."

Mekyla bent down and embraced her sister as she looked at the monitor jumping around every where. "Schonda, you're really not feeling those contractions are you?"

"Nope," Schonda said, as she lay back on the bed and scooped some ice out of her cup with a couple of fingers. She looked past Mekyla and noticed her door opening slowly.

Schonda's mom was the first to lean into the room, followed by Tere and Kimberly, all careful not to commit their selves to entering the room until they saw what state Schonda was in.

Mrs. Brinkley seemed relieved at what she saw. "Hey, we're back, how's my baby feeling?"

"I'm fine now that I've received the shot."

"Schonda, did anyone call Deon for you?" said Kimberly.

"Yes mama called him a little while ago. He had to take the kids to his mother's house, he'll be here. But you guys are interrupting. I want Mekyla to finish telling me about the guy in Austin."

All eyes were suddenly on Mekyla. She shook her head. "Uh-uh."

"What guy?" Mrs. Brinkley said, staring at Mekyla.

"Oh it was nothing. I met this guy during the book convention when I first went to Austin. And I was just getting ready to tell Schonda about my trip back to Austin."

"Okay." Mrs. Brinkley made herself comfortable in a chair. She began cleaning her teeth with a toothpick, but when Mekyla didn't say anything right away, her mom urged her on. "So, won't you tell us all about your trip?"

Mekyla gave Schonda the evil eye.

Schonda shrugged her shoulders. "What did I say?"

Mekyla slowly turned back to her mom. "Well, the reason I went back was to visit this gallery called Mitchie's there in Austin, yes that's why I went back. They had some wonderful art there, but this time was to . . .."

Mrs. Brinkley with a look of confusion as to what Mekyla was rambling about, the doctor came into the room with the nurse and greeted everyone. "I'm glad to see our mommy has so much support, but I'm going to have to ask everyone to leave except for the person who's going to assist with the delivery.

Mekyla smiled with relief. "Well mama, I guess I'll tell you guys about it later." She turned to Schonda. "Okay which side do you want me on and where is Deon big mouth?"

"Would you poke your head out in the hall and ask one of them to call and find out where he is please and then you can stand on my left."

Mekyla started for the door, but stopped when she saw Deon come into the room. "Well, look who it is. What's up future-brother-in-law? Are you ready to see this kid that I'm sure is going to eat you out of house and home?"

"I'm as ready as I'll ever be." He turned to Schonda and smiled while giving her a big kiss across the lips. "Hey baby, how are you doing?"

"I ready to get our third and final child out."

"I love you Schonda."

"I love you too Deon."

"Oh how sweet is that," said Mekyla. "Where's my love, I'm apart of this team."

"We love you too Mekyla," said Schonda as she took her sisters hand.

"Okay," said the doctor, as he began to spread Schonda's legs apart. "Get ready to give me a push."

"Okay, why are you squeezing my hand?" said Mekyla.

"Uh," said Schonda as she began to push.

"Schonda, you don't have to squeeze my hand for this

part. Remember? No pain."

"Give me another big push Schonda," said the doctor. "Mmmmm-uh."

Mekyla tried to pry loose her sister's hand. "Schonda, it's not necessary to squeeze so hard. Doc, please tell her not to squeeze the assistant's hand so hard."

The doctor ignored Mekyla and concentrated on his patient. "Okay, we're almost there Schonda. Okay this time, give me one more big push and we should have the little darling in the world."

"Oh my goodness," said Mekyla. "Get the kid out already before this girl pulls my fingers out of socket."

"Here comes the head, a little more Schonda, you can do it. Okay, you can stop pushing now," said the doctor. "You have yourself a beautiful baby girl." He lifted the baby up for Schonda to see.

"Ma'am," said the nurse. "Here are the scissors to cut the baby's cord."

"No thanks, I brought my own." Mekyla said as she began to reach for her scissors.

"Mekyla!" Schonda said with the little breath she had left in her.

"I'm kidding." Mekyla made a big show of taking the scissors from the nurse. "Thank you very much nurse. So where do I cut?"

"Right along here," she said, pointing to the spot.

Mekyla snipped right where the nurse was pointing. "Well, that's a crunchy sound. I guess that shot hasn't worn off so you can't feel it huh?" She looked over at Deon. "This doesn't mean that I'ma have to bond with this kid does it?"

"Yep, that's why I didn't want to cut the cord this time, because our other kids are killing me in expenses." But as the nurse handed the baby to Deon and he took her lovingly into his arms for the first time, his face glowed with pride.

"Can I leave now?" said Mekyla. "Because all of this afterbirth stuff is beginning to gross me out, I'll be outside waiting with everyone else and we'll come back in when you've gotten yourself together and cleaned all of that afterbirth off of your child with soap and water. You guys look terrible."

Schonda gave her sister a tired but satisfied smile. "Forget you Mekyla. Tell everyone to come in, in about five minutes."

"I will. Love you girl and congratulations guys."

"Thanks Mekyla," Deon said, still mesmerized by the new daughter in his arms.

Everyone stood up as Mekyla entered the waiting room. "Okay, well we did it. They are the proud parents of a beautiful baby cartoon."

"Mekyla!" Mrs. Brinkley said as she began to chuckle. "What did they have?"

"They have a beautiful baby girl."

"Can we go in now?" said Tere.

"They asked that we give them about five minutes."

Kimberly began to lie back down on the waiting room couch as she curled up. "I just want to get some sleep."

Mrs. Brinkley heaved a sigh. "It's good to have all of my girls here. Maybe not this way, but I'm glad you're all together." She looked at her watch. "It's getting close to seven. They should be getting Christy ready for her appointment with the psychiatrist."

"Oh yeah," said Mekyla. "Should we go up?"

Mrs. Brinkley thought for a moment. "No its best we wait until she comes out of it. Hopefully they'll release her right after."

"Hey mom, did you hear that storm that came through last night?"

"The windows are so tight in this hospital that I really couldn't hear it, but I did see the extra dark skies. The weather man was saying that conditions are going to be just right for tornados over the next couple of days."

"Well we're ready for any tornado," said Tere. "You know we had a storm shelter put in right beneath our house. You know, like the one in that movie *Panic Room*, but beneath?"

Kimberly laughed. "Tere, you're so afraid of tight places, I can just see you in the basement of your house. You'd have your cans of insect repellant fighting off the cobwebs made by all the spiders that have been making that nice cold block of concrete their little home for creating life."

"There are no spiders and insects in our basement – I mean storm shelter." Tere began to look around as if there were spiders closing in on her.

"And then," said Kimberly. "As she's in a state of panic, she stumbles down the stairs, bumps her head, passes out, but

41

through all that she still manages to get one squirt of the repellant to keep her safe from at least one of the bugs."

Tere shook her head. "What a vivid imagination Ms. Kimberly."

"Oh I'm not done. Then Ashton comes home to find Tere on the storm room floor with the can of repellant still in her hand, passed out cold, but safe from not only the storm, but also from the one bug that had the potential of crawling up her nose to restrict her breathing, in-turn causing her to die, not from the fall, but from only having the use of one nostril."

"Kimberly you are a sick girl," Tere said, squirming as a shiver went down her spine in reaction to her sister's creepy, silly story.

Everyone burst out laughing.

"Ha, ha," said Tere. "That's very funny." She pointed at Kimberly. "She'll probably be the first one over to our house to use the storm room."

"Heck yeah, if there's a storm and you have a safe place, you better believe I'll be there with my Westie."

Mekyla managed to stop laughing so that she could say goodbye to her family. "Okay guys, I'ma head to the house, I'm really tired and I have to work tomorrow. So give Schonda another kiss for me and I'll see you guys maybe later this afternoon. Mama would you or someone let me know when Christy is released?"

"Sure Mekyla, and say hello to Ian for me."

"I will mama. Bye guys."

"See ya Mekyla," Tere said as she turned to make her way to Schonda's room to see her newest baby niece.

CHAPTER FOURTEEN
FAMILY FIRST

Mekyla was relieved to have a few moments alone in the car and even better, to be on her way home to get some sleep in a nice comfortable bed. Halfway there her phone rang. She looked at the caller ID display, saw Jennifer's number and let out a big sigh.

"Hello?"

"Hello Mekyla, its Jennifer. Why haven't you returned

my calls?"

"I've been very busy and do you realize what time it is."

"I really need to talk to you about something and you haven't been returning my calls, which made me very worried. Can we meet sometime today?"

"No I can't today Jennifer, I've been running ever since the plane landed."

"What about tomorrow sometime, this is really important."

"I know what it's about Jennifer. Christy has already told me."

"I'm sure she didn't tell it right."

"I don't care if she told it while she was standing on her head. The only thing I'm concerned with right now is her getting better and out of the hospital."

"Hospital, Christy's in the hospital?"

"Yes Jennifer."

"Mekyla I didn't know that, is she okay and why is she in the hospital?

"Jennifer, now that's going to have to wait."

"Okay sure, I understand, but please hear me out as well okay, all I'm asking is that you hear me out."

"Okay Jennifer, but you must remember my family comes first always. You are a very dear friend, but don't put me in a position to choose, because you will get your feelings hurt."

"Ouch Mekyla, that kinda stung."

"This is why it's not a good idea for me to be talking to you right now. For one, I'm on the road, and two, I'm very tired. I'll call you when I'm ready okay?"

"Sure Mekyla, for whatever its worth, I'm very sorry to hear that Christy's in the hospital."

"Goodbye Jennifer," said Mekyla. She was about to hang up when she realized there was one more important thing to be said. "Oh wait. Jennifer? Are you there?"

"I'm still here."

"I just wanted to let you know that I'm really sorry I didn't get a chance to make it back for your grandmother's funeral."

"Thank you Mekyla, I'll talk to you later."

Sitting in her home, Jennifer hung up the phone and shook her head. Oh this is bad, she thought. This is not good at all.

"I'm home again finally." Mekyla said as she pulled into the garage. Not realizing that her vehicle was the only car in the garage, Mekyla walked through the kitchen and living room before going into the bedroom. She was relieved to see that Ian had already left for work. She tossed her keys on the dresser and fell onto the bed. She knew that eventually she'd have to get into the long talk Ian wanted to have. But at the moment all she wanted to do was sleep. Just a couple of hours without interruption and she'd be good to go. She hung her feet off the side of the bed and kicked off her shoes, then squirmed around, getting into just the right position, with the pillows just how she wanted them. She took one very deep breath and let it out slowly, letting all the stress drain out of her.

CHAPTER FIFTEEN
EVEN THROUGH OUR TRIALS, YOU'RE STILL THE ONE

Christy heard the door to her hospital room open and looked up to see Trey. "Hello."

Trey crossed the room slowly and took a seat in the chair. "Hello Christy," he said softly. "I miss you very much and I'm very sorry for everything that has happened. You must know that it's very hard for me to see the mother of my children in the hospital for something I've created."

"Were you here last night?"

"Yes, I didn't want to disturb you, I just wanted to be near you. In our thirteen years of marriage, a day has never passed that I didn't speak to you or see you that I can remember and I didn't want it to start now." Trey leaned forward and put his elbows on his knees and rubbed his forehead with the palms of his hands.

Christy leaned over and grabbed her purse from out of the nightstand and removed a piece of folded paper. "Trey, I want to share something with you that I wrote a few weeks ago."

Trey looked up at Christy and wiped tears from his face. "Sure Christy, I'd love to hear it."

"I titled it 'Twenty-one Questions.'"

Is this the beginning or is this the end?

Is it the way we disagree or when you get caught up and say it wasn't me?

Is this the beginning or is this the end?
When you make me smile and feel good inside and release all kinds of
feelings, I try hard to hide.
Is this the beginning or is this the end?
When I cry and you don't ask why or offer your sympathy or love. Is this a
sign for me to move on, or sent down from the heavens above?
Is this the beginning or is this the end?
What about when you hold me in your arms, the warmth of your skin
against mine, sending chills up and down my spine?"
Is this the beginning or is this the end?
When I say to myself, 'I can't take it anymore,' and pack your bags, sitting
them at the front door, but later that night, find myself saying, 'give me
more.'
Is this the beginning or is this the end?
On what grounds does the answer depend? Is the relationship over or
growing stronger again? To find out the answer can I wait much longer? Is
it wasted? Is patience the test? Some say counseling could fix this mess.
Hopefully not too much longer it will be, until I pass the lesson Gods been
teaching me.

Trey leaned all the way forward out of the chair and fell to his knees. He leaned against Christy's bed and began to cry uncontrollably.

Tears began to roll down Christy's face also as she rubbed the back of Trey's head in her lap.

"Trey, that poem was written before this, before I knew about your infidelities. You're not truly happy anymore in this marriage and I don't think I want to try for happiness anymore."

Trey suddenly jerked his head up and looked into Christy's eyes. "Christy, please before you say anything else, just think about it. I don't want to lose my family."

Christy leaned back against the headboard. She didn't speak a word. She just shook her head.

CHAPTER SIXTEEN
NO REST FOR THE WEARY

For a full thirty minutes she was in heaven. And then the phone rang.

She sighed again, this time in frustration. Slowly she

rolled over and grabbed the phone. "Hello," she said in the most pleasant voice she could manage.

"Mekyla, this is mom. Christy called down a little while ago to ask that we all be present for what she has to say."

"Uh – but that's okay mom, I already know."

"She asked me to call you."

Mekyla sat up straight. "Is everything okay?"

"She won't say. I know you're tired sweetie, and that's why I made you my last call."

She swung her legs out of bed and grabbed her shoes. "Mama, I'm on my way."

She punched the button to hang up her mom's call and opened the line again. She dialed Ian's work number, wondering why everything in her world was so out of control and how much more she was going to be able to take. Every time she felt she'd reached her limit, some new catastrophe came along to push her just a little farther. She held the phone with her shoulder and tugged her shoes back on.

"Dow Chemicals, this is Swayla."

Mekyla was up off the bed and grabbing for her keys. "Hello Swayla, this is Mekyla. Is Ian available?"

"He's in a meeting right now Mekyla."

"This early, he's in a meeting."

"Did you want me to interrupt it?"

"No I'm sorry, I'm just thinking out loud, just tell him that I called, thank you."

"I will and you're welcome."

Mekyla hung the phone up and hurried out the door and jumped into her car.

Mrs. Brinkley leaned back in her chair in the waiting room. "Okay Mekyla should be here in about fifteen minutes or so."

Kimberly looked at her watch.

"How are we going to do this?" said Tere. "Will Schonda go to Christy's room or will Christy come down to Schonda's room?"

Mrs. Brinkley nodded her head. "Schonda's probably still very sore. I'll just go up and get Christy."

Christy thought if Trey hadn't had a chair to fall into he'd be laid out on the floor. Her statement had hit him hard. But she couldn't help that. It was time for her to take care of herself, at least, as far as she could under the circumstances. "Trey, if you don't mind, I'd like to talk to my family alone."

Trey struggled into a more upright position in the chair. "I understand. But please take your time with the decision you're making. That's all that I ask of you."

"How are the kids?"

"They're still at my parent's house. I was hoping to be able to bring them *and* you home today so that you could see each other. They're very worried about you."

"I have to see the psychiatrist before I can leave. Would you bring them up here to see me?"

Trey hesitated for a moment. "Are you sure you want them up here?"

"Yes, if you don't mind."

"Okay," he said, as he stood up. "I'll go right now."

"Thank you Trey."

He started for the door, but turned back with a worried look on his face.

Christy heard footsteps and saw her mom appear in the doorway behind Trey.

"Well, hello stranger," said her mom.

Trey turned to the door. "Hello Mrs. Brinkley."

"Were you working a lot or something?"

"Oh no, I was just, I was . . . ."

"Mom, he was here last night," said Christy. "He stayed overnight with me."

"Oh, we must have just missed each other. Trey you look as tired as I feel. How are my grand kids?"

"They're fine Mrs. Brinkley. As a matter of fact, I'm on my way to get them so they can see their mom."

Mrs. Brinkley frowned. "Is that a good idea? Christy you won't you be released today?"

"I don't think so mom. I'll talk to you about it in a little bit okay. Trey, I'll see you in a bit. Mom, I guess we're just waiting on the others?"

"Well Schonda had her baby. She's worn out and sore, so I came to bring you down to her room for our little talk."

Christy's tired eyes brightened a bit. "Schonda had the baby? What did she have?"

"A girl, she had a girl."

"Mrs. Brinkley, please congratulate Deon and Schonda for me," said Trey. "And Christy I'll see you in about an hour."

"Okay Trey."

They watched him go and then Mrs. Brinkley turned to her daughter. "What do we need to do to get ready to go down there?

"Mom if you would just grab my clothes out of the closet, then I can follow you to Schonda's room." She twisted around and sat on the edge of the bed.

"I'm glad to finally see Trey here, looked like he'd been crying." She pointed toward the door he'd just left through. "Now that's a man that truly loves his wife." Remarking as she held up Christy's white blouse and navy pants.

"Thanks mom."

As Mrs. Brinkley held the blouse and helped Christy get her arms through the sleeves, she replied. "You never did say why you took those pills."

"I know mom, we'll talk about it when I get to Schonda's room."

"Why am I always grouped with your sisters? I'm your mother, some things you can just say to me."

Christy leaned back onto the edge of the bed as she put her feet through the legs of her pants. "I know mama and I do. Just not this time, okay." She stood up. "Let's go see my niece. We just have to stop at the nurses' station so you can sign me out."

"Sign you out? Why, do they think you're crazy or something?"

Christy shrugged. "That could be a yes."

As Mekyla made her way to Schonda's room, "Okay," she said, putting her hands on her hips. "I just want to know if anybody really loves me, because if you did, you would have allowed me get at least two hours of sleep before calling me."

"Hey sis, this was Christy's call," said Schonda.

"Hello Schonda, how are you feeling?"

"I feel like I just delivered a six pound kid."

"Where's Deon?"

"He's down with the baby. He'll be all up in her face until she starts mixing up her days and nights, then he'll start to fade away."

Kimberly was sitting on the corner of the bed and Mekyla sat down with her back to her. "Kimberly, please rub my neck."

"I'm just as tired as you are. Will you rub mine?"

"No."

"No?" Kimberly playfully slapped her sister on the back. "You should have waited at least a minute before blurting out that answer."

"Tere?" said Mekyla, nodding to her other sister. "Rub my neck please."

"Sure Mekyla, for a dollar," Tere said, as she began to message Mekyla's neck.

"Ooh, that feels good. Down a little lower in the middle please. Yep, that's it."

"Can I be next?" said Christy, standing in the doorway with their mom.

"Hey sis, how do you feel?" asked Mekyla.

"I'm feeling fair to partly cloudy. Hey Schonda, where's the newest addition to the family?"

"She's down in her room with her daddy."

"So what did you guys name her?"

"We haven't decided on one yet." She held up a hand, "Actually, let me rephrase that. We haven't agreed on one yet."

"Oh I see. Well the name Erin comes to my mind."

"Erin, that's a very pretty name. I'll talk with Deon about it. Thanks Christy."

"So what's this news that you have?" Schonda said, fluffing up her pillows to get comfortable for the big announcement.

Christy sat down in a straight-backed chair and took a deep breath. "Okay, everyone knows I took too many pills, but you don't know why." She thought for a moment. "And actually, you know what? I don't want to begin with that. Mama, have a seat." She patted the seat of the recliner next to her.

Her mom eased herself down into the chair, not taking her eyes off of Christy. "Now you're scaring me," she said.

"Just tell us what it is baby."

Christy's heart was beating fast. She knew there was no easy way to say what she had to say, so she just blurted it out. "Well, I have cancer."

"What?" Shouted her mom, while springing to her feet.

"This is the reason why my hair has been coming out. I've had cancer over six months that I know of."

Mrs. Brinkley sat down heavily again. A very still silence descended on the room. With their heads bowed, Christy's mother and sisters began to wipe the heavy tears from their faces.

Christy shook her head. "Guys I'm at peace with this. It took me a long time to get here, that's why it took me so long to tell you."

Mekyla's head shot up. "Peace with it? What do you mean? They're going to do something for you, right? The doctors are going to – to – to help you or Chemo right."

All eyes were on Christy again.

She held up her hands, trying to calm everyone. "No, because the cancer has begun to spread throughout my body and I don't know if I want Chemo." She leaned over and gave her mom a big hug. Her sisters were instantly on their feet and huddled together around Christy in one enormous embrace.

"Christy," said her mom. "Either I'm coming to your house to live or you're coming to mine."

"Sure mom, I figured that's how you would respond and that going to be just fine."

"I love you Christy,"

"I love you too Tere. Don't cry guys. We're never on our time; it is and has always been, on the Big Man's time."

The group hug began to break up, only so that someone could find plenty of tissue.

"I tell you what guys," said Christy. "After my kids leave, I'd love to sit around with everyone and just reminisce about the times before we had to worry about terrorist or people being killed by the thousands on our own soil." As she smiled and looked at her mom, she said, "Mom will go home and bake a batch of your chocolate chip cookies and give us each one and let us watch you eat the rest for old time sake."

Everyone laughed through their tears.

Christy dried her eyes and stood up. "I've got to get back to my room," she said. "If I don't make it to my appointment, the psychiatrist will set off the escape alarm. And mom signed me out, so she's going to be in a lot of trouble." Besides, Trey is bringing the kids up to see me in a few minutes. She smiled and waved goodbye to everyone as she walked towards the door.

"Christy, now that was a beautiful exit," said Mekyla. "But, call me when you're done with your appointment. She held her mom's hand as they all watched Christy go.

"Well mom," said Schonda, dabbing at her eyes with a tissue. "You better scoot if you're going to have those cookies done by lunch time."

"Schonda don't be silly. I really don't feel like I should leave right now. I have this funny feeling way down in my soul, that something isn't right."

"Of course you feel that way mama," said Tere. "We're all feeling a little weird after what Christy just said."

"No, I mean something else, something even more than that."

"We're all going to get through this," said Kimberly. "We just need to stick together as a family and especially stick close to Christy right now. You don't need to make cookies if you don't want to and I don't mean to be ordering you around, but I think everyone would agree with me that you need to go home and get some rest."

"Mama, Kimberly's right," said Schonda. "Besides I'm getting ready to check out in the next couple of hours or so. Maybe you can take me home, take a shower and then come back up here. What do you think?"

"That shouldn't take any more than a couple of hours, right? I guess I can manage that."

"Good," said Mekyla. "You need a break and unless somebody else has a crisis for me to deal with at the moment, I'm going to head home and get at least two or three hours of sleep before going into the office to check on things." She looked from face to face to see if there were any objections. "Good," she said, not hearing any objections. "I'm wiped out; love you guys and I'll see you later."

"Okay Mekyla," said Schonda. "Drive safe."

CHAPTER EIGHTEEN
HE GAVE ME THESE TEARS TO CRY

As Christy approached her room she saw Trey stick his head out the door, then look over his shoulder into the room. "Hey kids," he said. "Here comes your mom down the hall." He looked back at her and smiled. "Hello baby, how was your visit?"

"It went well. I'm sorry, I took so long, but I stopped by the nursery to see Schonda's baby."

She looked past Trey into the room and waved at her kids. They waved back and smiled. She led Trey out into the hallway. She had to struggle to hold back her tears as she spoke to him, trying to keep up her courage for what she was about to do. "Do you think I could have a moment alone with the kids?"

Trey hesitated just from the look that Christy had on her face, but then nodded, "Sure, you know that's not a problem. I'll be right out here if you need anything."

She watched him start down the hall and then she went in to face her children. She hugged them then sat down in one of the chairs. "Okay kids, I want you to listen to me very carefully. I love each and every one of you very much. Mommy's fine, it's just that I took too many pills at one time, but I'm okay now. I may just be tired for a while and I won't be able to tell you to do all the things you need to do. So I want you guys to listen to your big sister when she's trying to tell you to do things the right way. I don't want you fussing at each other, because you're a family. Family sticks together always."

In sync the children replied, "Yes ma'am."

She could see the hints of concern in her children's faces. "Everyone come closer to me and give me a big bear hug, one that I can keep for a long time." As she hugged her kids she shut her eyes tight and fought back the tears of love for her children. When she felt she'd swallowed all her tears as she stood up and smiled down at her kids. "Okay, so let's go out there with your dad." The kids started running down the hall. "Slow down guys, before you hurt yourselves."

She walked slowly down the hall with her arms around

their daughter, who has become this beautiful young girl growing rapidly before her eyes and joined the rest of the family. "Thanks again Trey, for bringing the kids up," she said. "I know that's something you would normally be against."

"Christy," said Trey, leaning in close to have a private word with her. "I want you to know that I've loved you for as far as I can remember, even in bad times such as this, I've loved you. I will never stop loving you as long as there's breath in my body and we will get through this."

"Trey," she whispered back. "It's okay if you decide to be with Jennifer when I'm gone. "Jennifer and I may have had our differences in the past and the present. But it's not about us anymore. There's a kid involved and it's your responsibility to take care of that child if he's yours."

Trey shook his head. "I'm not going to be with Jennifer, you're all I want. You're all I ever wanted, that other thing just happened. It was a mistake I made and I'm truly sorry for that. I'll never leave my family and that thought has never even entered my mind."

Christy nodded. "I don't mean to rush you off, but I need to get ready for my appointment with the psychiatrist."

Trey took a couple of steps back. The kids had wandered off towards the elevator. "Okay, I'll see you tonight or tomorrow, whenever they release you; if that's okay."

"Sure, you'll see me tomorrow, kiss my kids for me." Christy made eye contact with her kids and waved goodbye to them. She walked back to her room, closed the door and finally released the tears she'd been trying so desperately to keep locked up.

She cried for a few moments, feeling both the pain and relief of finally letting go. But eventually she realized she had to get herself together, she had things to do. She went into the bathroom in her room and splashed cold water on her face and gathered her thoughts for a minute, trying to picture the layout of the hospital in her mind. When she was satisfied that she had it all worked out, she grabbed her purse.

She hurried down the hall to the nurses' station waving the purse. "Excuse me nurse, but my husband left this behind. He was supposed to take it with him. If I hurry around the corner, I can catch them at the elevator."

The nurse looked worried. "But Mrs. Love, I'm not supposed to let you leave without being signed out by someone else."

"It will only take me a moment if I'm able to catch them at the elevator."

"Okay, but please hurry. My shift ends in about five minutes." The nurse looked at her watch.

"I will hurry, thank you."

She burst through the double doors and around the corner to the elevators. She pushed the button several times quickly. She looked back to make sure no one was behind her. She pushed the elevator button several more times. "Come on, come on, come on," she said. She heard the ding of the elevator's arrival and looked over her shoulder again. The doors opened. The elevator was empty. She hesitated, thinking about the psychiatrist, her appointment, her family, and then her children. As she took it all in, she stepped into the elevator and pressed the button for the ground floor.

CHAPTER NINETEEN
SEEKING MY QUIET COMA

Ian walked through the house looking for Mekyla and finally found her in the bedroom. "Mekyla," he called out as he walked through the door. He stopped quickly when he saw that her eyes were closed. He realized she'd been so tired that she must have fallen asleep before she could even get out of her clothes.

He tiptoed to the closet to grab his gym bag so he could go work out for a couple of hours. As quietly as he could, he began rummaging through the closet for all his gear.

"Ian," said the sleepy voice from behind him. "Hey."

Ian turned, cringing. "I'm sorry baby; I was trying not to wake you. I left the office early, to get a jump on my workout so that I could get back here and start dinner, before it got too late. So, you just go back to sleep. I should be back in a couple of hours or so. Is everybody okay?"

Mekyla yawned and stretched. "Yes, Schonda should be released in another hour or so, and Christy should be at her appointment with the psychiatrist right about now, pleading her case for release." She rolled over to face the other side of the room.

"I'm going to go baby, so that you can get some rest," Ian said. He gazed at her form on the bed for another moment, certain that he'd made the right choice to give them another chance.

CHAPTER TWENTY
WITH EVERY SETTING COMES A DAWN

Mrs. Brinkley pushed Schonda's wheelchair slowly through the lobby of the hospital toward the front doors. She looked over her daughter's shoulder at the baby in her arms. "Let me hold my grandchild."

Schonda looked back and smirked. "Mom, you can't hold her and push me at the same time."

"Oh I know, you can get up and walk, I won't tell."

"You will have plenty of time to bond with her."

"I hope Deon found my car to put the car seat in there."

"I'm sure he did mom."

The automatic doors opened and Mrs. Brinkley guided the wheelchair through them and into the fresh air. "Wow, I haven't been outside of those walls since I arrived at the hospital a couple of days ago."

"Mom, technically it won't be a couple of days until in the morning."

"Well it felt like a week. And then to discover one of my daughters has cancer. Schonda I didn't really want to say this in front of Christy, but this is going to be the death of me as I watch my child go through something so painful."

"I know mom, I know." Schonda adjusted her baby's little cap, wanting to keep her safe and secure from the world outside. "But she's going to be fine. She'll beat this cancer. She better beat this cancer."

As Schonda and her mother both sank deep into reflection, the whole world seemed to fall silent around them.

CHAPTER TWENTY-ONE
A CRY FOR HELP

Mekyla groped for the ringing phone without even

opening her eyes. She knocked it to the floor and had to lean over the edge of the bed to get it. "Hello."

"Mekyla, its Christy."

Mekyla smiled, still not opening her eyes. "Christy, sweetie, how are you feeling?"

"I'm okay Mekyla. I wanted to say goodbye to you. I would love to say goodbye to everyone but mom. How do you say goodbye to your mom?"

"Christy, what are you talking about? You just say goodbye, but where are you going to have to say goodbye?"

"Not just goodbye Mekyla, I mean my final goodbye."

Suddenly all the last remnants of sleep were gone from Mekyla. She sat bolt upright in bed, eyes wide open now. "What do you mean your final goodbye?" She scrambled out of bed and began looking for her car keys. "Just sit tight for a few minutes; I'm on my way back down there, okay."

"I'm not there anymore Mekyla. I've checked myself into a hotel," said Christy, slurring her speech a little.

"Don't play with me Christy, have you gone mad? Don't do this to me or yourself, tell me where you are okay." Mekyla checked the caller ID, but all the readout said was, "Unavailable." Mekyla said to herself in a quit panic.

"I wanted to call you and visit with you, because your voice calms my soul."

Mekyla nodded, grabbing her keys off the dresser and shoving them into her pocket. "Okay, that's good, that's good Christy. Just tell me where you are and I'll come over and we can have another sister to sister talk." There was a pause. "I want to see you Christy, please tell me where you are okay?"

"Trey brought the kids up to see me and – oh I think you already know that huh?" Christy's voice was growing softer. "They look so sweet and innocent, if I had to single out one great thing from my marriage, it would be those beautiful children me and Trey made." Christy said, as she rolled onto her back with her head dangling from the edge of the bed while looking up at the ceiling.

With tears streaming down her face, Mekyla began to put on her shoes. "Yes, I definitely have to agree with you on that one sis, you guys did give mama some beautiful grandchildren."

"You know a grandmother's love is precious, but a mother's love is untouchable."

"That's so true Christy, and that's why your kids need you to nurture and watch them grow. And I need you, what about the value of a sister's love, how about that, huh."

Rolling back onto her side as she attempted to move in a better position on the bed, Christy replied, "I'm getting really sleepy Mekyla, okay come and get me."

"Okay baby, just tell me where you are."

"I'm right here," said Christy attempting to point at her own self.

But Mekyla could barely here her, "What did you take to make you so sleepy?"

"Mekyla I'm scared and I'm so sleepy and tired."

"Christy, please tell me where you are. Did you say you where at a hotel, which hotel are you in, do you know what color the building is?" There was more silence on the line. "Christy are you there, Christy please, continue to talk to me so that I can come and get you."

"Ask that taxi guy, he would know, he was so nice to me. Please come and get me now okay, I don't want to die here. Hurry-up Mekyla, I know you'll find me, you're my big sister." Christy said in a quiet whisper, as the phone rolled from her fingertips.

Mekyla heard the phone clatter to the floor. "Christy, Christy, oh my God, are you there?" She hesitated to hang up the phone, afraid to lose that only connection she knew she had to Christy, with one last attempt to call out to Christy, "Christy," there was no answer and then she hung up the line to dial 911, but her hands were trembling. She paused and took a deep breath. "Calm down," she whispered to herself. "Okay, please calm down Mekyla and call for help," After dialing 911 there was this person that came on the line that startled Mekyla, "Hello."

"Are you calling for police or fire?" the voice on the other end again attempted to ask.

"I need the police please."

"Would this be for emergency or non emergency police?"

"Emergency, this is an emergency."

"One moment please, while I connect you."

Mekyla turned her eyes to the heavens and uttered a silent prayer as she waited for a few seconds that seemed like hours.

"Officer Johnson," a voice finally said. "How may I help you?"

"My sister has left the hospital and I believe she called me from a hotel, maybe nearby."

"Your sister, is she in danger?"

"Yes, she was admitted to the hospital yesterday morning for taking an overdose of pills. She was supposed to be under watch, but she left the hospital somehow and has checked herself into a hotel."

"Do you feel she might take more pills?" Officer Johnson said as he took notes to what was being said.

"Yes I believe she already has taken more pills. She called me a few minutes ago and towards the end of our conversation, she mentioned being very sleepy and that she didn't want to die and then she dropped the phone. Officer Johnson, please help me find my sister."

"What's your name?"

"My name is Mekyla Williams." Mekyla left the house and started for her SUV.

"Ms. Williams, I need for you to give me the name of the hospital and your sister's name."

"She was in St. John's hospital and her name is Christy, Christy Love. She's my sister and not the actress; she married into that last name. I love her very much and she wants me to come and get her, please help me." She said as she got into her SUV and cranked up the engine.

"We'll find your sister Ms. Williams. What floor was Ms. Love on?"

"She was on the twelfth floor. Do you want me to meet you there?"

"Yes, I should be there in about ten minutes."

"I'm on my way Officer Johnson, goodbye."

Mekyla pulled her SUV out of the driveway and headed for the hospital. She scanned the names programmed in her cell phone for Christy's and hit dial.

Trey answered the phone on the forth ring. "Hello."

"Hello Trey, this is Mekyla."

"Hey, how's it going Mekyla."

"Trey, Christy has left the hospital."

"They've released her already; I thought she would call me to pick her up."

"No, she left on her own."

58

"So is she over at your place, did she want me to come and get her?"

"Trey I don't know where she is. She called me from some hotel and she was really disoriented. I think she's taken more pills, because she said she was very sleepy and then she dropped the phone."

"And she didn't say what hotel she was in?"

"No she said to ask the taxi driver."

"Where are you now Mekyla?"

"I'm on my way up to the hospital to meet with an Officer Johnson. He's going to help us find her."

"Okay listen," said Trey with panic creeping into his voice. "Give me time to drop the kids off at my mother's and I'll be right there."

"Okay, drive careful Trey."

"I will."

Mekyla found Tere's number in her cell phone and punched dial. As soon as Tere answered, Mekyla blurted out the details as clearly as she could. "Tere, this is Mekyla. I need for you to call mama and tell her that Christy has left the hospital on her own and is in trouble. Wait, no don't tell her that, just go by her house and pick her up. She had mentioned going back up to the hospital, so just tell her you wanted to ride with her."

"Hold on, if Christy has left the hospital, why are we going there, shouldn't we go to where she is?"

"We can't, that's what I'm trying to tell you, she's missing."

"What, what do you mean 'missing'?"

"Tere please let me explain when you get to the hospital and call Kimberly too please." Mekyla closed her flipped phone and gunned the car through a yellow light.

CHAPTER TWENTY-TWO
DESPERATION EQUALS PANIC

Mekyla dialed Ian's phone, but there was no answer. She then hit auto dial to his work number as she pulled into the hospital parking lot.

"Dow Chemicals, this is Swayla."

"Good afternoon Swayla, this is Mekyla. May I speak with Ian?"

"Hello Mekyla. Ian's on the plant floor somewhere – or – no, actually he left early."

"Oh, what am I doing?" said Mekyla. "That's right. Could you please check the company gym for me to see if he's there, thanks again Swayla, oh and Swayla, when you locate him, have him call me on my cell phone please."

"Is everything alright Mekyla?"

"Yes, but if you would get that done for me I would really appreciate it."

"Sure, I'm on my way down now."

"Goodbye Swayla. Of course he'll turn his cell phone off at a time I needed him the most." Mekyla said to herself as she scanned the isles for a parking space not too far from the front doors. "Alright, I can't believe I got so lucky."

Throwing the car into park, she jumped out and began to run through the entrance of the hospital and headed for the elevators. The elevator seemed to take forever to get to the twelfth floor and when the doors finally opened, Mekyla rushed out, rounded to corner, shoved through the double doors and started talking before she'd even reached the nurses' station.

"Hello, nurse? I'm Christy Love's sister, has Officer Johnson made it up here yet? I'm supposed to meet him."

"Yes he has, he's down this way waiting for you." The nurse began to lead the way down the hall. "I wanted to say that we're very sorry for allowing Mrs. Love to leave the hospital. She said she was just going to give something to her husband around the corner and that she'd be right back."

"Sure, okay," said Mekyla, spotting the man in uniform and losing all interest in what the nurse was saying. "Hello Officer Johnson, my name is Mekyla Williams, I'm the one that spoke with you on the phone about my sister, Christy Love, what do we do next?"

"I need for you to tell me what your sister was wearing, how tall, the color of her hair, eyes and skin tone."

"I don't really know what she was wearing, but my other sister that's on her way up here would be able to help you with that. Christy has brown hair and eyes, medium skin color; she's about five foot-five inches, and about a hundred and thirty-five pounds."

"Did she have access to a car here at the hospital?

"No she was brought in by ambulance, but on the phone she mentioned a taxi driver." Mekyla heard footsteps behind her and turned to see Tere hurrying down the hall with their mom. "Here's my sister and our mother now." Mekyla beckoned them to hurry. "Tere, would you please sit with Officer Johnson and give him the rest of the information that he needs on Christy and I'll go with mama and talk to her."

Mekyla took her mother by the arm and led her away so that they could have some privacy.

"What's going on Mekyla," said her mother. "Why are you guys being so mysterious? And why is there an officer here, did she do something, is she in trouble for taking those pills?"

Mekyla took Mrs. Brinkley into Christy's room and led her to a chair. She pulled up the other chair, sat down and took her mother's hand. "Mama, Christy is missing, she has left the hospital and at the moment we don't know where she is."

"Christy should be in her appointment, Mekyla."

"She didn't make the appointment and she left the hospital, I know because she called me from a hotel."

"Okay well what hotel, let's just go over there and get my baby."

"It's not that simple mom. We don't know which hotel and we believe she has taken more pills." Mekyla began to bite at the knuckles of her free hand, trying to fight back the tears.

"Mekyla, are you telling me that my baby has taken more pills and that her life may be in even greater danger and we don't know where she is?"

"Yes ma'am."

"Oh somebody's gonna find my baby, where's that officer?" Mrs. Brinkley sprang to her feet and started back down the hall.

Mekyla caught up with her. "Okay mama, I know that you're upset, but we're going to need to be very level headed and give them all the help they need to find Christy."

"Tere," said Mekyla. "Where's Officer Johnson?"

"He's meeting with Christy's doctor."

"Did he mention what they were going to do next, have they found out which taxi driver took Christy to the hotel?"

"No and no Mekyla, he said for us to wait right here. But I did hear him on his radio requesting backup and to have detectives dispatched out. Deployed, I don't know which word he used, but it was something to that effect."

Mekyla pointed down the hall. "Here comes Christy's doctor now."

The doctor strode down the hall and put a hand on Mekyla's shoulder. "Hello, I know this is tough for all of you. Let's go into Mrs. Love's room where we can sit and have some privacy."

As they made their way back to Christy's room, the doctor explained as much of the situation as he knew. "I was telling Officer Johnson that the pills Mrs. Love has taken may have been a prescription medication called Elavil. This is something that I've prescribed to Mrs. Love once before. And if that's true, they would pose an even bigger threat than the pain pills she took before.

"Elavil, please explain what that's used for," said Mekyla.

"Elavil is an anti-depressant. If she's taken, let's say 300 to 500 milligrams then I'm afraid we're only working with five to seven hours."

"And then what?" said Mrs. Brinkley. "What do you mean five to seven hours?"

"It's a fairly powerful drug. Even in prescribed doses, the drug has some risks. It may cause drowsiness, enticholinergic effects, stroke, coma, confusion, extrapyramical symptoms, hypo or hypertension, nausea, or fatigue." He shrugged and shook his head. "But if your daughter has abused the medication, if she's taken it in the larger doses I mentioned, I'm sorry to say Mrs. Brinkley that after five to seven hours all of her organs will shut down."

Mrs. Brinkley slumped in her chair and closed her eyes.

The doctor reached out and put a hand on her shoulder. "My staff and the police are doing everything possible to locate the taxi company that picked her up here, and they're calling all of the surrounding hotels."

"Can I help, doctor?" said Mekyla. "I want to help." She stared into the doctor's eyes, exhausted, but unable to sit idly by and just wait.

"Sure, if you'll follow me, I'll take you to the head nurse who's overseeing our efforts."

Mekyla turned to Tere. "Will you stay with mama please?"

"No, I want to help as well."

"Who's gonna stay with mama?"

Mrs. Brinkley shook her head. "I'll be fine Mekyla. Both of you go ahead."

"No," said Mekyla. "You come with us. I don't want to lose you as well."

"You're not going to lose me Mekyla."

"You don't understand, I have to find her mama. She asked me to come and get her and I can't go and get her if I don't have someone to take care of you."

"Okay I'm coming with you Mekyla. We're going to find her, I know we will."

"Here's Kimberly," said Tere. "She can stay with mama."

"Hey guys, what's going on? I get this urgent text message from Tere just telling me to come to the hospital." Kimberly raised her hands in confusion. "So would somebody please fill me in?"

"Mama will fill you in okay?" said Mekyla. "Come on Tere, let's follow the doc."

"Mekyla," said Mrs. Brinkley.

Mekyla stopped in her tracks and looked over her shoulder. "Yes?"

"What time was it when she called you?"

"You really shouldn't worry about that right now mom."

"What time was it Mekyla?"

"I don't remember mom."

"Give me the time Mekyla."

"One, it was around one." Mekyla said as she closed her eyes remembering how much time they had to work with.

CHAPTER TWENTY-THREE
A ROOM FILLED WITH LOVE; YET SO EMPTY

Trey came through the double doors on the twelfth floor just in time to see Mrs. Brinkley and Kimberly going into Christy's room. Eyes full of hope that maybe Christy was back in her room and everything was all right. But when he arrived to her room, he saw that the bed was empty. "Mrs. Brinkley," he said. "I got here as fast as I could. What's going on, has Christy called again or do we now know where she is?"

"No Trey, there's no word yet."

"Would somebody please tell me what's going on here?" said Kimberly.

"Of course Kimberly, both of you guys come over here and have a seat."

Trey and Kimberly sat down as Mrs. Brinkley began to explain as much as she knew.

CHAPTER TWENTY-FOUR
COUNTING THE MINUTES

Tere did the math in her head and then said what neither she nor Mekyla wanted to admit was true. "So if she called you around 1:00 and took the pills maybe thirty minutes before she passed out and dropped the phone, then we only have about four or five hours from now to find her."

"Yep, that just about sums it up." Mekyla said just as her cell phone started to ring. In a rush to pull it from her pocket, it dropped to the floor. "Hold on," Mekyla cried out just in case it was Christy calling again. She looked at the caller ID readout and scoffed in frustration. "Excuse me, Tere. I need to take this call from Ian."

She answered the phone and could immediately hear the worry in Ian's voice.

"Mekyla, is everything okay?"

Mekyla pushed the hair back from her forehead as she half whispered into the phone, hearing the panic in her own voice. "No it's not. I can't find Christy and I don't know what this is going to do to mom. I've got to find my sister because she asked me to."

"Mekyla, I'm not sure I follow. Has Christy disappeared from the hospital, is that what I'm hearing you say?"

"Yes. She – I got a call, and . . .."

"All right," said Ian. "Just stay calm. Where are you now?"

"I'm at the hospital."

"I'm on my way."

"Okay," Mekyla said, as she hung up the phone. Wiping a few tears from her face she heard a loud voice coming from the other room. She tucked the phone into her pocket and made her way toward the voice.

"Who let my sister leave anyway?" Tere said in a very loud manner to the nurse. "And why haven't we found the hotel or the taxi guy yet. If something happens to my sister everyone in this hospital – "

"Tere," said Mekyla. "This is not the time for that. We need to stay focused on finding Christy. I apologize for our outburst, but we're very upset right now and we're very scared. So if you would please continue to help us find our sister we would greatly appreciate it."

Mekyla closed her eyes and tried to keep it together. She felt someone take both her hands and opened her eyes to see Trey standing before her.

"Okay," he said. "What can I do to help?"

She took a deep breath and gestured to the people on the phones. "Well, what these kind people are doing is calling around to all of the hotels and taxi companies trying to make a connection to Christy."

"Where do I start to call from?"

"Right over here Trey." She led him to an available phone. I guess we find out what hotels and taxi services they've already called and go from there."

"For what it's worth, I love my wife and kids. I did something very stupid and it will – "

"Trey, I'm not the one to forgive you. Let's find my sister and go from there, okay?"

Trey gave a big sigh and nodded.

CHAPTER TWENTY-FIVE
BEGINNING TO WHAT END

Junior stuck his head back into his room. Everything was packed, but Jennifer was still sitting there on the edge of the bed. "Jennifer, are you ready to go?" he said as she seemed lost in thought. "Jennifer?"

She looked up, "Yeah and why are you shouting?"

"Are you ready to go?"

"I'm ready if you're ready," she said as she stood up. "Hey Junior, have you ever thought about changing your name from Brent Elliott, because you can, you know."

Junior furrowed his brow. "Why would I do that? That's my father's name, the name that was given to me. That's a stupid question to ask somebody, let's go."

"Yeah, okay, of course that was a silly thing to ask you. So are you excited about college?"

"Yep, I'm ready to be on my own you know? It's like I grew up in a house with two mothers. You ride me harder than mom sometimes."

"It's only because I love you very much and because I want you to be successful in everything you set out to do."

Junior stacked two boxes and snatched them up off the floor. "Grab that bag for me sis."

"Sure, is that everything?" She picked up the bag and followed Junior out the door. "I'm really going to miss you. I'll probably move out and buy my own house and you know you will always be welcome in my house."

"I know Jennifer and I appreciate that. You've been a very cool sister. I've always felt a motherly love from you. I know that sounds weird, but it's true." He led the way out the front door and glanced back over his shoulder as he walked. "I felt you were more like a mom to me than our own mom. Thanks for keeping me on the straight and narrow." He crammed the boxes into the trunk of Jennifer's car with the other things that were already there. Then he took the bag from Jennifer and tossed it on top of everything and slammed the lid down.

Jennifer fished the keys out of her purse. "Hop in big head and let's get you to Oklahoma City. Oklahoma University is going to be proud to get a young man like you."

"Thanks sis."

CHAPTER TWENTY-SIX
ANGEL SENT

Mekyla practically fell out of her chair when she heard what the man was telling her. "What?" she shouted. "You remember my sister, where did you drop her off at?" She was aware that all eyes were on her now as she listened to the man on the other end of the line.

The voice said on the other end of the phone. "If this is

the young lady I picked up around noon from St. John Hospital, then I took her to the Ramada Inn on Fifty-First Street."

"Thank you very much for your time, but hold the line while someone take your name okay." Mekyla said as she hung up the phone and jumped out of her chair. "Hey guys, I think I may have something. That was possibly the taxi driver, uh, that drove Christy to the hotel. He said he dropped off a young woman fitting Christy's description at the Ramada Inn on Fifty-First Street." She looked at her watch. "It's almost five o'clock, guys, Tere, Trey, let's find Officer Johnson."

Tere grabbed up a phone. "I'll call the hotel to make sure this is the one Christy checked into."

"That's a good idea, Tere; I'll be back with Officer Johnson." She hurried out the door and called over her shoulder, "Trey, you come with me."

Around the corner she found Officer Johnson working a phone himself. She leaned both hands on the desk he was working from. "We may have a lead. She may be at the Ramada Inn on Fifty-First Street, Tere's checking that right now."

Officer Johnson followed her back to the office Tere was in.

"What did you find out Tere?"

Tere listened intently to what she was hearing on the phone and held up a finger to quiet everyone. "Okay," she said into the phone and then she heaved a heavy sigh and put her hand over the receiver. "Okay guys, here's what I got. The hotel has put me on hold to go up to the room that this woman checked into. If it's Christy, she didn't check in under her real name, but we'll know in a couple of minutes."

After that, no one said a word. Mekyla looked at the clock, bit her finger and searched Tere's eyes, looking for a sign that she was getting some news from the other end of the phone line.

"Hello," said Tere at last, "Yes?"

Everyone stared at her as she listened to the other end of the line.

"Oh, my God," she said. "You don't understand if she's not answering the door it's because she's overdosed on pills and has passed out. Please get your manager to open the door to that room now, this is a matter of life or death."

There was another brief pause and then Tere yelled,

"Wait?"

"What?" said Trey, "What's happening Tere?"

"They put me on hold again," Saying with a look of frustration and water forming in her eyes.

Trey put his hands on top of his head and looked up at the ceiling. "Come on, come on, come on," he said.

"What?" Tere said with panic in her voice. "We're here at the hospital right now and the police are with us, I'm sending them right now." She hung up the phone.

"What?" again Trey cried out.

"There's a lady in the room unconscious and unresponsive, it's got to be Christy."

Before Tere had even finished speaking, in the background Officer Johnson was on his radio requesting police and medical response to the Ramada Inn at 3131 East Fifty-First Street.

One of the nurses who'd been helping with the search called down to the emergency room and told them to be ready for the arrival of an OD victim.

"Officer Johnson," said Mekyla. "How long is it going to take to get to my sister?"

"They usually have a three minute response time, but that can vary with traffic."

"What do we do now?"

"You wait here and if you're a praying family you pray that we made it in time," he said as he headed for the door.

"Okay guys, let's go down and wait with mama and Kimberly," Tere said as she put one arm around Mekyla's waist and took Trey by the hand. "Come on brother-in-law."

As the three of them entered the room, the girls began to speak at the same time.

"What," Said their mom? "Slow down, I can't make out a word of what you're saying."

"Mom," said Mekyla. "We found her, we found Christy and they're picking her up from the hotel as we speak."
Mrs. Brinkley looked up toward heaven and clasped her hands together.
Mekyla threw her arms around her mom and held her tight.
Tere put her arms around both of them.
As Trey returned from the nurses' station with an update on what was going on. He'd advised everyone that Christy had just arrived to ER.

"Okay guys," said Mekyla. "Everything's going to be fine, she's here now. And they're going to make everything okay."

"Everything's okay?" said a voice from the doorway.

Mekyla turned to see Ian standing there, with a look of deep concern on his face.

"I came just as soon as I could. Did I hear you say everything's okay?"

"I hope so, she arrived just a few minutes ago."

"That's great, right, so are they bringing her up?"

"No, she's being treated in the emergency room now, she took more pills Ian."

Mekyla put her hands to her face, wondering what she could do at this point, wanting to help in any way she could.

Ian rubbed her back and looked around the room. He nodded to Trey. "Trey, how's it going man?"

"I'm doing okay Ian, thanks for asking," Trey said, as he slid down the wall taking a seat on the floor of the hospital room.

CHAPTER TWENTY-SEVEN
CONNECTIONS

Jennifer sat in her car, watching the newly arriving students unload their belongings in front of the dorms. She dialed Mekyla's number and looked around for Junior to give him one last wave before leaving. But he'd gone inside and was probably already busy making friends with everybody. She heard Mekyla's voicemail message and sighed in frustration. "Hello, Mekyla, its Jennifer. I just wanted to let you know I just dropped Junior off at college and I didn't tell him about Trey and I'm not going to. Please call me so that we can talk, I really miss you and I'm very sorry for everything. Okay, well you know how to reach me. Talk to you later, bye and I love you."

CHAPTER TWENTY-EIGHT
FROM OUR HEARTS TO YOUR HANDS

Kimberly was running back into the hospital room, cut the corner too close and hit her shoulder on the doorway. "Ouch, that hurt," she said and began rubbing her shoulder. "Hey everyone, the doctor is on his way down the hall right now."

The room fell completely silent as everyone listened to the approaching footsteps and watched as the doctor entered the room.

He had a medical chart with him, but he didn't bother to refer to it as he spoke. "Hello everyone, we treated Christy in the Emergency Room. We pumped her stomach and gave her a number of medications intravenously to try to counteract what she'd taken. The truth is that we simply didn't get to her in time. I'm sorry to have to tell you – "

Before he could finish his announcement, the room erupted in screams and tears. Mrs. Brinkley who had stood before the doctor began to slump. Trey grabbed her and put his arms around her. Mekyla fell to her hands and knees and began beating the floor in rage. Ian dropped to one knee beside her and put his hands on her shoulders. Tere and Kimberly threw their arms around each other and held on tight.

"I'm very sorry everyone," said the doctor. "I'm very sorry for your loss." He drifted slowly out of the room to give the family their privacy.

After a time, Kimberly still sniffling picked up the bedside phone and called Schonda and Deon.

"Schonda, this is Kimberly."

"Oh hey Kimberly, how's everything going?"

"I have some bad news Schonda, we lost Christy." Kimberly sat down on the bed, cradling the phone with her shoulder.

"Kimberly, don't be silly, we didn't *lose* Christy, she may be going through some tough times right now, but she'll come out of it. We just need to give her time and our love and support."

As Kimberly listened to her sister that didn't understand what she was trying to say, she began to ask for Deon. "Schonda, where is Deon?"

"He's in there with the baby."

"Schonda, listen to me, we lost Christy, she's no longer with us."

Kimberly listened to the silence on the other end of the

phone. Finally she heard the phone clatter to the floor.

"Schonda are you okay? Schonda, please talk to me," Kimberly said she looked over at Tere coming towards her to give that warm hug that she needed.

Miles away, Deon picked up the phone off the floor. "Schonda, what's wrong?" he said. He put the phone to his ear, but it was dead. He hung it up and turned to Schonda again. "Baby, what's wrong?"

"We lost Christy."

"What, what are you saying, she passed? But I thought she was recovering."

Schonda shrugged her shoulders and shook her head as she began to release her tears.

"Baby, I'm so sorry, I'm so sorry for your loss." He put his arms around her. "What do you want to do, where is everyone?"

"I believe they're at the hospital, I would like for you to take me there please."

"Of course baby let me just call my folks so they can come over and watch the kids for us."

"Mrs. Brinkley, I'm very sorry," said Ashton as he became aware of what just happened. "She will be truly missed." He extended an arm to his wife, "Tere, come here sweetie." He closed his arms as she stepped into his embrace.

"Is Schonda on her way up, anybody?" Mekyla said, as she looked around the room.

Kimberly nodded. "Yes, I called her a little while ago. I'm sure she's on her way now."

"Thanks Kimberly, I guess we'll just sit and wait for her before we go up and say our goodbyes to Christy."

"Mekyla, did you need me to get you anything to drink?"

Mekyla shook her head. "Wait, you know what, actually could you please grab me a cup of water?"

"Sure." He looked around the room. "Would anybody else like anything to drink?"

"No thanks Ian," Trey said as he sat in a corner with his head in his hands.

"I'll take some water," said Kimberly.

"Sure, I tell you what, I'll just bring several bottles of water back."

"Thanks," Mekyla said as she managed a half smile. "This is such a weird feeling that I'm undergoing. It's like this really isn't happening, you know, um, like a test of my endurance. I am so overwhelmed and frustrated with everything right now. I just want that doctor to walk back in here and say that they made a mistake, that Christy is just fine."

"Mama," Schonda said as she entered into the hospital room. She took one look at the bed where Christy had been recovering and began to cry. She spread her arms wide and hurried to her mother.

"Hello baby," said Mrs. Brinkley while embracing her daughter. "I just don't understand why my baby would do this to herself." She looked past Schonda. "Trey, do you know why she would do this to herself. Did she say anything to you about what was going on in her mind?"

Mekyla gave Schonda a hug as she spoke. "Mom, are you up to seeing Christy at this time?

"Mekyla, why do you keep doing that? Every time I ask my son-in-law a question, you somehow block it."

"I don't know why I do that mom, but I do know that he's under as much stress as we are and feels the loss just as much. Not only has he lost his wife, but he's lost the mother of his children as well. And I just feel this isn't the time to have him answer for Christy's choices in life."

Mrs. Brinkley thought about Mekyla's wisdom and nodded. "I understand and I'm sorry Trey. It's just that I don't really know how I feel about everything right now."

Trey shook his head. "Mrs. Brinkley no offense taken, your loss is greater than mine. You lost your daughter today and I strongly believe that there is no love greater than a mother's love. So with that said, let's go up and see the lady we all loved so deeply in our own way." When he saw Mrs. Brinkley bow her head, Trey looked over at Mekyla and mouthed the words, "Thank you."

When Officer Johnson had finished all the necessary paper work, he walked over to Mekyla and handed her a piece of paper. "This was found next to Ms. Love. I thought you would like to have it."

Mekyla's heart skipped a beat as she took the paper, sensing what it might be. "Thank you very much for all of your assistance and genuine concern of my family."

"Not a problem, I just hate that it ended up on a sad note. And I'm very sorry for your family's loss."

Mekyla watched Officer Johnson walk away as she tried to gather herself. With a look of hesitation Mekyla knew she had a piece of her beloved sister last thoughts in her hand.

"What is it that you have there Mekyla?" Mrs. Brinkley said as she approached.

"It appears to be a letter from Christy. I guess I'll just read it in front of the whole family, if it's okay with you."

Mrs. Brinkley took a deep breath and struggled to hold back the tears. "Let's get everyone together in this waiting room over here."

CHAPTER TWENTY-NINE
THE SILENT VOICE

Mekyla stood before the people she loved and looked into their faces. As she saw Christy in their eyes, she swallowed hard once then looked down at the paper in her hands. "It says,"

I'm ready for this to be over; I'm ready for the end.
I feel like I have no one on whom I can depend.

She paused, looked at her family again, and then continued to read. "Then it says,"

To my children,
I will remember your smiling faces now and forevermore.
Your laughter, your hugs, and your kisses I will forever adore.
I won't be there throughout your lives, but I was there at the start.
My love will live on forevermore in each of your tender hearts.

She paused to dab at her eyes with a tissue. "Then it reads,"

To my sis, thank you for sharing your kindness with me
Without you in my life who would I be?
Watch over my children and teach them to love
Be kind and caring as you were to me, as I watch you from above.
I'm tired of living; I'm tired of my life
And it seems all I ever go through is commotion and strife.
I'm sorry it had to end this way, if I can explain it I will.
Or I can end it all right now with this little white pill.
How many will it take, maybe two, or three, or five?
What if my brilliant plan didn't work and I lay here still alive?

I'm waiting for Mekyla to save me. Saying, "You can work your problems
out."
Maybe now they'll listen and understand what my life was all about.
Do I want to end it all, well now I have no choice?
Please listen well and hear me now, now that I have no voice.
I love you mama, now you can see and think of me as your little girl always.
Christy.

As they all listened with heads bowed and tears streaming down their faces, the room grew even more silent.

Mekyla collapsed into a chair. It was a moment before she could speak again. "If you guys don't mind, I think I'll go in later and see Christy I'm just not up to it right now." She looked down at the letter and knew that she would have to read it again in private. "Ian," she said, looking up. "Would you please go with my mom?"

Ian put a hand on her shoulder. "Yeah baby, but are you going to be all right if I leave you here alone?"

"Yes, I'll be fine, I just need a little time to myself that's all."

"Okay, I'll be back in a little bit." Ian took hold of Mrs. Brinkley's arm and began to lead her to view Christy's body.

"Alright guys, see you later okay." Mekyla took her cell phone out of her purse and dialed a number. On the third ring a familiar and cherished voice answered. "Termaine," she said, "This is mom."

"Oh, hey mom, I was just bragging to Shandalyn about your spaghetti. I was also saying that you haven't cooked it for me in a while."

Mekyla smiled sadly. "I see, well I'm going to have to cook you some real soon."

"Yeah," said Termaine. "You know I have to show off my mom's great cooking."

"Sweetie, the reason I called was to tell you that your Aunt Christy passed away."

There was a pause and then Termaine blurted out, "My Aunt Christy died, why?"

"She had cancer, yeah, she had cancer."

"Aw man, I had no idea she was sick like that. Where are you?"

"We're all up here at the hospital."

"I'm on my way up there."

"I'll be at the house in another hour or so, why don't you just meet me there."

"I'll be there, is grandma and Uncle Trey there?"

"Yes, they're both here."

"Mom, are you going to be all right?"

Mekyla gritted her teeth, fighting back the tears, proud of her son's love. "Yes, really, I'm fine. You know what, I think I'm going to sneak out and go to the house right now. I really don't think I can take anymore of this hospital scene." Mekyla grabbed her purse and headed for the elevator.

"That's probably a good idea, what about grandma?"

"Ian and Trey are with her. Plus, your aunts Schonda, Kimberly and Tere are here as well with your uncles, with the exception of Kimberly of course."

"Okay, well drive safe and I'll see you at the house in just a little bit."

"I will, love ya. I would love to see that grandbaby of mine."

"I'll see what I can do about that; see you in a bit mom."

CHAPTER THIRTY
WHICH ILLUSION IS THIS?

"Babe," called Ian as he entered the house. "Where are you?"

"I'm in the kitchen."

"Something smells really good," He said as he approached Mekyla in the kitchen with a soft, sad smile on his face. "Your mother is at her house safe and your aunt is there with her."

"Thank you very much for doing that Ian."

"Not a problem. Why are you cooking?"

"I spoke with Termaine a little while ago, he talked about bragging on my spaghetti to his girlfriend. He's going to stop by and I wanted to surprise him with spaghetti."

"Do you need any help?"

"No thank you, I need something to keep my mind occupied."

"Well I'ma wash some of this dirt off of me, okay? Have you called your office to let Marie know that you're not coming in at all today?"

"No I haven't, she's not expecting me for another couple of days, I think. I'll call her later." Mekyla said as she began to sample the sauce.

Mekyla heard the door open and smiled, knowing who it was.

"Hello," called Termaine. "Are you home?"

"Of course," said Mekyla. "I'm in the kitchen."

Termaine found his way into the kitchen hand in hand with his latest girlfriend. Hello mom, you remember Shandalyn."

"Yes of course, hello Shandalyn."

"Hello Ms. Williams."

"Is that spaghetti sauce I smell?" Termaine said as he made his way to the stove to lift up the covered dish.

"Yep."

"Are you making enough for guests?"

"Yep," Mekyla said, as she stirred the sauce. "Come over and give me a hug, it seems like forever since I've seen you."

"Well, the last time was when we went to eat at Zios just last week."

"Yes, of course, we need to do that more often."

"That's what you said when we were there."

"Life is really short, we must hang out more." Mekyla said, as she gazed into the pot of sauce.

"Where's Ian?"

"He should be coming out of the shower any time now."

"Ms. Williams, did you need any help?" Shandalyn asked, with a very soft smile on her face.

"Oh that's sweet of you to ask, but I think I've got everything covered for now. I think there's some soda in the refrigerator if you guys would like something to drink."

Termaine put his hands on his mother's shoulders as she added the sautéed chunks of bell pepper and onions with the ground beef to the sauce. "So, when will the funeral be held for Aunt Christy?"

"We'll probably have the services on Monday. But first we need to get together and make the arrangements. On your way home today, why don't you go by and see your grandmother, she'll like that."

"I will mom." Termaine turned and saw Ian stroll into the kitchen. "Hey Ian, how's it going?"

"As well as can be expected Termaine." He turned to Termaine's girlfriend. "I remember your face."

"Hello, I'm Shandalyn. We met at the barbeque at Termaine's Aunt Tere's house."

"So you guys are having dinner with us tonight, don't be a stranger Termaine, stop by more often."

"I know I should and I will," Termaine said, as he gazed at the framed photos of the family.

"I think your mom is almost done cooking, let's go in and have a seat at the dinner table."

CHAPTER THIRTY-ONE
WHERE DO I START

Trey stood on the front porch of his parents' house and took a deep breath. There was no easy way to do what he was about to do, but after everything that had happened, nothing was easy about his life anymore. He opened the door and forged ahead.

"Hello mom."

"Hello Trey, the kids are in their room playing. Did you want me to get them?"

"No not right now." He sat on the edge of the sofa and put his elbows on his knees.

"How's Christy, is everything okay?"

"No ma'am. Where's Dad?"

His mom furrowed her brow. "He's in the bedroom, would you like for me to get him dear?"

"Yes ma'am."

"Okay, hold on." She pushed herself up out of her chair and went to look for her husband, glancing back at Trey as she went. "Papa, come into the living room, Trey wants to talk with us."

When she returned to the living room, she was ringing her hands in anticipation of what her son was going to say. "Are you hungry dear?"

"Yes and no. I believe I'm very hungry, but at the same time I don't really have an appetite."

His father strolled into the living room just then.

"Hello dad."

"Hi son, how's that wife of yours?"

Trey bowed his head. "Both of you please have a seat."

Trey waited until his parents sat down. "Mom, dad, Christy – she didn't – she didn't . . .." Trey squirmed in his seat, trying to finish his words.

"Son," said his father. "What's the matter, what's wrong, is Christy okay?"

As hard as he tried to fight back the tears he couldn't do it. He sobbed loudly, covered his mouth with his hand and shuddered as the tears rolled down his cheeks. "Christy didn't make it, we lost her this evening."

"Oh dear," said his mom. "How and why Trey did this take a turn for the worst? I thought she was going to be fine."

Trey shielded his eyes with his hand. "Ma, I don't know how to tell the kids."

"Oh my Lord, yes dear, the kids." His mom glanced over her shoulder toward the room where the kids were playing. She could hear their laughter. She shook here head. "That's going to be so difficult. But you're the only person who should deliver such news. Just be very gentle with them." She looked at her son. "And maybe you should wait for a while. Maybe after you calm down a little bit and clean yourself up."

"No," he said, suddenly pushing up off the couch. "I don't feel like I should delay this. I just took them to see their mom earlier today. She asked to see them, this just isn't right." Trey began to make his way to the kids' room, and then he stopped. He turned one way, then another. "You know what; I can't do this right now. Mom dad, would you mind if the kids stayed overnight and I tell them tomorrow?"

"No, of course not Trey," said his father. "Of course they should stay."

Trey began making his way to the front door. "Thanks, I'm just going to head for the house."

As Trey left his parents' house, his phone began to ring. He pulled it out of his pocket. "Hello?"

"Hello Trey, this is Jennifer."

Trey looked up at the sky and sighed. "Not now Jennifer."

"Please don't hang up the phone. I just wanted to call and tell you that I didn't tell my son about me or you. I dropped him off at college a few hours ago."

"This is not the time Jennifer."

"That's all that I wanted to say. So you and Christy can hopefully rebuild your lives and I won't interfere anymore."

Trey shook his head. "Jennifer, Christy died today."

"What?" Jennifer said.

It was a moment before Trey could speak again. "Yes, she took her life earlier this afternoon."

"I am so sorry. It's my fault, oh no. I know this is my fault."

"No it's not. Christy and I were having problems before you. And it was an accumulation of things. No one thing could have caused her to take her life."

"Where are you Trey?"

"I'm just now leaving my parents house."

"Can we meet?"

"I don't think that would be a good idea. I left the kids with my folks. I just want to be alone."

"You shouldn't be alone right now Trey. It doesn't have to be at our regular spot. Have you had dinner?"

"No, but I don't really feel like being out right now."

"How about if I came over and cooked for you."

Trey thought for a minute. "Sure, fine, I'll see you in a little bit Jennifer." He said as he took a moment to look back at his parent's house with one foot in his vehicle.

"I'll come right over."

"And do me a favor," said Trey. "Pull your car into the garage and push the button to close it, please."

"Sure," said Jennifer.

CHAPTER THIRTY-TWO
TWO WRONGS CAN'T MAKE THIS RIGHT

Trey struggled to open his eyes and saw the early morning light streaming into his bedroom.

"Good morning," said a voice.

He looked up and saw Jennifer gathering up her things. "Hey," he said. "What time is it?"

"It's close to seven-thirty. I need to head to the house and change for work."

"This probably shouldn't happen again."

"Why not Trey, it's not like we haven't done it before. I

know that you're going to need time to mourn for Christy, but let's not brush aside what we have. It feels so good and so right."

"We'll talk about it again at a later time. Right now I need to get myself together and find the words to explain this to my kids." Trey rolled out of bed and started to make his way to the bathroom to take a shower.

"Trey, would you like for me to join you or are you going to see me out?"

Trey froze halfway to the bathroom. "No, I'm sorry. Let me let you out." He put on his robe and accompanied Jennifer down the stairs.

At the foot of the stairs, Jennifer walked straight to the front door and put her hand on the knob.

"Here," said Trey. "Go out through the garage."

"Oh yeah, I forgot I parked in there."

Trey opened the door for her and stepped aside. "See ya Jennifer."

As soon as he closed the door to the garage he was startled by the doorbell.

"Now who could that be?"

He made his way to the front door and opened it. "Mrs. Brinkley, I didn't know you were coming by this morning."

Mrs. Brinkley furrowed her brow and cocked her head. "What's that noise I hear?"

"Oh, it's the garage door, come on in." Trey led the way to the kitchen. He glanced over his shoulder. "Have you had your coffee yet this morning?"

"Yes, I've been up since five o'clock. I stopped by to ask if you started the arrangements for Christy's funeral."

As Trey entered the kitchen and grabbed a filter for the coffee maker he shrugged and gave a soft smile. "No, I haven't. I figured you would want to be a part of the whole process. I'll take care of everything as far as the financial side is concerned."

"Did my daughter have a will?"

Trey began to scoop coffee into the filter. "Yes she did, our lawyer has all of that information."

"And was there a life insurance policy?"

He nodded as he counted out the last scoop. "Yes, we have life insurance on both of us, but with how she died may cause a problem."

"Okay, well the girls and I will make all of the arrangements, pending your approval to the financial part of course. Are my grandchildren here?"

"No, they're still at my mom's house. I'll tell them today."

"Would you like for me to be there with you?"

"No, my parents will be there, but thanks anyway."

"When this is all over, I would still like to have a talk with you about what it was that my daughter was going through to make her do this to herself."

Trey put his hands in the pockets of his robe. "Sure, when everything settles we'll talk."

"Well, I won't keep you."

Trey nodded. "Thanks for stopping by Mrs. Brinkley."

He escorted her out the front door. As Mrs. Brinkley walked to her car she looked into the open garage, then she looked back at Trey. "We'll keep you posted on the arrangements."

"Okay," said Trey, but it was only a whisper, barely loud enough for her to hear. He closed the door with his back and then slowly slid down the door into a squatting position. He rested his forehead in the palms of his hands. "What have I done?" he said out loud. "What am I doing?" And the tears began to fall from his eyes.

CHAPTER THIRTY-THREE
A HOUSE OR A HOME

Mekyla opened her eyes and looked up at the ceiling above the couch. She heard Ian moving around in the room.

"Good morning Mekyla."

"Good morning Ian." she said, rubbing her eyes.

"You know you don't have to sleep out here."

"I know, but we've had this conversation Ian. I just feel its best right now."

Ian sighed. "I said that I forgive you. Let's just wipe the slate clean and start fresh."

"We can't wipe the slate clean," she said, sitting up on the edge of the couch. "I did what I did for a reason. Maybe what we have is not enough, I don't know. I just know that I need time. And if it's too difficult for you to have me staying here while I go through what I'm going through, I can go back to my house." She smirked, "If there's a house left."

"No," said Ian, crossing his arms. "I would rather you stay here and we work it out together." He looked down at Mekyla. "What are your plans today?"

"I'ma go in and check on Marie briefly." She yawned. "I'm going to clear off some of the stuff that's waiting on my desk and then take the rest of the day off." She struggled up off the couch and started for the bathroom.

When she emerged, teeth brushed, face splashed with cool water, Ian was hard at work in the kitchen.

"I'm making some toast and eggs. Did you want some, but we're out of sausage and bacon."

"Yes please, but no eggs, I'll just take toast."

"I've started heating some water for your tea if you wanted to fix a cup."

"Tell you what," she said, making her way into the kitchen. "You make the toast and eggs and I'll fix your coffee and my tea, how about that?"

Ian smiled. "That sounds like team work to me." Then he worked at the skillet for a moment. "Promise me something Mekyla," he said.

"What?"

"When all the arrangements for Christy are taken care of, can we please sit down and have a talk?"

Mekyla pushed her hair back from her forehead. "Sure, that's fair," she said.

Ian nodded.

"I guess I should call Jennifer back," said Mekyla. "She's been blowing up my cell phone."

"Are you guys not speaking?"

"No, but yes, I don't know what to do with this whole Trey thing."

Ian furrowed his brow and lifted the spatula out off the pan. "What Trey thing?"

"Oh, that's right. I haven't had a chance to tell you why Christy was in the hospital. Christy found out that Jennifer and Trey were having an affair."

"What?" Ian turned completely away from the stove.

"The first overdose of pills that she took was when she first found out."

"You're telling me – wait – Trey and Jennifer? Who would have thought those two would have affair? How did she find out?"

"That evening right before it happened, Trey and Christy were at home. Trey's cell phone started ringing while he was out of the room and Christy decided to answer it. On the other end of the line was Jennifer. Christy asked her why she was calling Trey and she said that her son was Trey's."

Ian took the skillet off the burner and tossed the spatula into it. "Hold on," he said. "What, what son?"

"I just found out about it myself. Apparently her mother has been playing the role of 'Mommy' all these years Jennifer couldn't or wouldn't or was too scared to change it. Then she decided she'd had enough and was going to confront the father, who lived in Louisiana. A guy she went to college with."

Ian rubbed his face with his hand. "Wait a minute, you lost me."

"I know," said Mekyla, holding up her hands. "But just listen. She went all the way to Louisiana only to discover that the guy she went to see was here in Tulsa. You remember the lady that had the cashmere sweater on at your basketball game?"

Ian furrowed his brow. "No."

"It's okay Ian."

Ian shrugged. "Okay, so go on."

"Okay well, it turns out that she was the wife of this guy that Jennifer went looking for. So she comes back to Tulsa and confronts the guy and he takes one look at the picture of Jennifer's son and tells her it's not my son. He looks nothing like him."

"Well?" said Ian, hanging on every word. "Did he?"

"After carefully looking at the photo herself, Jennifer realized that this guy wasn't her son's father. Then somehow I guess she decided to claim that he was Trey's son. Some of this information I got from Jennifer and some I received from Christy. So who knows what the whole story is, other than Jennifer, I guess. But I haven't had the chance or really even wanted to speak with her right now. I mean, apparently she was playing my sister Christy. And now Christy's dead. So how am I supposed to deal with that?"

"Do you blame Jennifer?"

"Well no and yes. I don't really know what to feel about

Jennifer. I just know that it wasn't time to talk to her."

Ian raised his eyebrows. "And you're ready now?"

"I think so. I need to do something with all these feelings that I have. Ian I miss my sister, I really miss my sister."

"I know baby, come here." Ian stepped toward her and put his arms around her. "I want you to know that I'm going to be by your side every step of the way. And I want you to also know that I'm not going to take advantage of this time to make us close again. It's just that I love you and when you hurt, I hurt."

Mekyla put her arms around Ian and allowed him to hold her close.

"I'm heading out for work now," said Ian after a long moment. He glanced over at the stove. "Have some of whatever you want on the stove," he said. "And call me if you need me, okay?"

"Okay."

CHAPTER THIRTY-FOUR
CLOSURE IS SO FINAL

Mrs. Brinkley sat in her home with most of her daughter's gathered around her. "I went by Trey's house this morning to find out what he wanted to do as far as the arrangements for Christy were concerned," she said. "He said for us to make all of the arrangements and that the expenses will all be taken care of."

"This feels weird," said Tere. "I don't know if I've fully digested this whole thing about Christy being gone. She has no more life. How final is that? Not to mention the kids. What about the kids?"

Mrs. Brinkley stared out the window and spoke softly, distantly. "Well Tere, they do still have a father. Who could be more capable of providing for them?"

"Yes, maybe financially," said Tere. "But who's going to see about their emotional needs?"

"That's something that we're all going to look after."

CHAPTER THIRTY-FIVE
WHAT A VACATION

Mekyla pushed open the door to the office and waved to Marie. "Good morning, Marie," she said.

Marie's eyes brightened. "Mekyla, it's good to have you back. How was your vacation?"

Mekyla tilted her head to the side. "It was cut kind of short. I was called back home early from a trip because one of my sisters became ill."

Marie frowned. "Oh no, I'm sorry to hear that. It must have been serious if it interrupted your trip."

Mekyla bowed her head. "Yes this was pretty serious. The end result was that we lost our sister."

Marie put her hands to her mouth. "Oh Mekyla, I'm sorry to hear that."

Mekyla nodded. "Thank you," she said. "So what I'm going to do is close out some of the stuff that's on my desk and get out of here. You can always reach me on my cell phone if you need me. And City Farm Agent Taylor Ellis would be more than willing to help me out if needed."

"Of course," said Marie. "Anything pressing that I should know about?"

Mekyla thought for a moment. "No, just the normal business, there's nothing pressing I can think of at this time."

"Wow, I'm really sorry for your loss. All of your sisters were fairly young, right?"

"Yes, they're all under forty."

"Can I help in any way?"

"Thanks for the offer. I'll let you know."

Mekyla headed for her office and immediately picked up the phone to call Taylor Ellis. As she waited for an answer, she shuffled through the paperwork on her desk.

"Thank you for calling City Farm, Taylor Ellis' office, how may I help you today?"

"Good morning, is Taylor available?"

"Yes, may I tell her whose calling?"

"Sure, this is Mekyla Williams."

"Mekyla, I thought that was you. Hold the line please."

"Thank you."

Mekyla continued to look through the mail as she waited

to be transferred.

"What's happening, vacationer," said Taylor, bright and cheery.

Mekyla dropped the mail and sighed. "Well Taylor, first I'd like to thank you for stopping in every now and then to check on my office."

"Oh, you're welcome. Who knows, I might need that favor in the near future myself."

Mekyla smiled. "Well you know you got it. Second, I wanted to let you know that while I was on vacation, we lost my sister Christy."

There was a pause on the line. "Christy?" Taylor finally said. "I remember Christy. Oh my. I'm very sorry to hear that Mekyla. Is there anything I can do to make this process easier for you and your family?"

"Well I do have one more favor to ask of you."

"Name it."

"I'm just asking for more of what you've been doing for me. I'm going to need to spend time with my mom and my sisters to complete the arrangements for Christy."

"I totally understand. Consider me there."

"Thanks very much Taylor."

"No problem."

"So did anything exciting happen during your visits to my office?"

"No, nothing out of the ordinary happened. You have a very loyal and smart staff person. She's a keeper."

Mekyla smiled. "I know. Thank you."

"Other than all these handsome men coming into the office asking only for you, I would say nothing out of the ordinary happened."

Mekyla giggled into the phone. "Well, what can I say?"

"There was this one man that was especially handsome. Oh I can't remember his name, but he left his card. You should see it on your desk. Wow! Talk about a man you want as the entrée and the desert. He would be it."

"Okay enough about my book of business. I guess I'll find that card under all of this other paperwork."

"I'm sure you will."

"Okay. Again thanks a lot for all of your help."

"You're welcome," said Taylor, then she softened her voice. "And hey," she said. "Be sure to let me know when the services are."

"I will. Goodbye Taylor."

Marie lifted her hands off the keyboard and picked up the phone. "Good morning, City Farm Insurance, Mekyla Williams's office."

"Hello Marie. It's Termaine, is my mom available?"

"Yeah, hold on Termaine." Marie put the call on hold and buzzed Mekyla. "I know you said hold all calls, but this is your son," she said.

"Of course," said Mekyla. "I'll take it." She pressed the button for line two and greeted her son. "Hey baby, how did you know I was here?"

Termaine scoffed. "You're always in one of three places, home, work, or in your car."

Mekyla laughed. "Okay, I'll give you that. What's going on?"

"I'm here at grandma's house. You'll never guess who's here."

"No, I probably can't. So let's say you won this round."

"Uncle Stoney is here."

Mekyla's jaw dropped. "Wow! So Stoney's in town? It's been a long time since he set foot on Oklahoma soil. But he's not your uncle son, he's your second cousin."

"Saying uncle Stoney sounds better to me. He got in early this morning. Did you wanta talk to him?"

"No, not just yet, but I'm on my way over there."

"Okay, see you when you get here."

Mekyla hung up the phone and walked into the outer office. "Marie, have you been getting your breaks and lunches okay?" she said.

"Yes, whenever Taylor hasn't been here I just lock up and go next door to the deli."

Mekyla cringed. "I'm really sorry for the inconvenience. You know what, give me some names of qualified candidates to come in and work on a part-time basis okay."

Marie shook her head. "Sure Mekyla, I'll get right on that and it's not that I'm overwhelmed with work, but I would like the company. It gets really boring at times."

"Okay, continue doing what you've done all last week and I'll see you on Monday. Have good weekend."

"Your family will be in my prayers."

"Thank you Marie."

Termaine plopped down into an easy chair across from the couch were Uncle Stoney was sitting. "That was moms on the phone just now. She's headed this way."

Uncle Stoney smiled. "Brick House Mekyla. And they didn't call her that because she was a brick house. And that's not that she's not attractive, but we nicknamed her that because she always had a brick wall up that no man could penetrate. That Mekyla was a debater."

"Was?" said Termaine. "She still is." He and Uncle Stoney both laughed.

"So Termaine, what are you doing for yourself?"

"I'm in security."

"Meaning Brinks Security, or rent–a-cop-Barney-Fife security?"

"Oh you got jokes, huh, Unc? Well, I'm not with Brinks, so I guess I'm like the Barney Fife security, whatever that is."

"You don't know anything about The Andy Griffith Show?"

"Oh yeah, I remember seeing that show once on the TV Land channel. You know the channel where they show all the stuff in black and white."

"Man, somebody's getting old and it's not me. I like living in denial."

Termaine chuckled. "I've heard moms and grandma talk about all of the trouble you use to get into."

"I guess that took up about five years of your life just in conversation." They both laughed again.

"Well, they did have a lot of stories and I guess they were really funny. Because after each story, they would laugh until tears rolled down their faces."

"Did they tell you about the time I went to jail? Well, about one of the times I went to jail. I can't remember why I went in this particular time. But I do remember that I was drunker than drunk."

"Unc, once you're drunk, you don't get any drunker."

"Well, let's just say, twenty-first century person, that

back in my day there were other levels of being drunk and I would be at the highest level there was. You could have sat me beside a bum on the street and wouldn't take a second look."

"Okay," said Termaine. "I get the picture."

"So, like I was saying. I was taken to jail late one evening and was in a cell with another drunk. We started to scuffle, right. Neither one of us was really doing anything to hurt the other one. The next morning at breakfast, I guess he still had some stuff on his mind, because before I knew it I was hit upside the head with a metal tray."

"What? He hit you with a tray?"

"Yep, and I was still hung over. Imagine the new headache I had."

"Unc, man, that's crazy."

"Termaine, son, would you go into the kitchen and fix me a drink."

"Sure, Unc, what do you want? I believe grandma has some Pepsi, some juice and maybe some Kool-Aid made up."

"I'll definitely have the Pepsi, but with some of that E & J your grandmother has hidden up in the cabinet. Because I know she keeps the Remi or Covoisier in a nice safe spot."

Just then Termaine's grandmother walked into the living room.

"Grandma, do you have liquor in your house?" said Termaine.

"For me, no. But I do keep an occasional bottle here for my guests. Why?"

"Unc wanted me to fix him a drink."

She nodded. "For Stoney, there's some E & J in the cabinet." She headed into the kitchen to find the bottle. The doorbell rang. "Stoney," she called back into the living room. "Get the door."

Termaine took the bottle of E & J that his grandmother handed him.

"Thanks grandma," he said as he turned to see who had just come in. "Hey, what's up Ashton, Auntie Tere, how are you doing?"

"Hey Termaine," said Ashton, peering past him into the living room. "I can't call it right now. Tere, is that your cousin Stoney over there?"

"Yep," said Termaine. "Sure is."

Ashton walked into the living room with a big smile on his face. "Hey, Stoney, when did you get in man, I'm Ashton, seen pictures of you and we spoke on the phone a couple of times. It's finally nice to meet you."

"I arrived this morning." He shook Ashton's hand and then gave Tere a hug. "Look at you Tere. The last time I saw you, you were this dorky little girl with glasses. Now look at you. Marriage agrees with you."

"Well thank you Stoney, I guess." said Tere, with a doubtful look on her face. "Don't get me started on you. Based on the stories Mekyla and Christy use to tell, you don't stand a chance against me."

"Did I hear my name?" said Mekyla, coming into the living room. "What's happening Stoney, it's really good to see your handsome face."

"What's happening cuz, you're looking terrible, but you smell good."

"Forget you. You just don't know the half of what I've been going through."

"Well, I can imagine."

Mekyla put her arms around Termaine. "Hello son, any luck on me seeing that grandbaby of mine?"

Termaine shrugged. "I don't know. Her mom still won't let me see her the way I want to. But I'm getting ready to solve all of that."

"Oh yeah, well as long as it's legal and safe, I'm behind you one hundred percent."

"I'm glad you said that, because I am going to need your help."

"I knew that. I was just wondering when you'd ask. We'll talk about this at a later date, okay?"

"Thanks mom. I love you."

"I love you too son."

"Where's Ian?"

"He should be at work."

"He's a pretty cool guy. I know I don't tell you that often, but I like Ian."

Mekyla furrowed her brow, not knowing quite how to respond to that statement, but she just nodded her head in agreement.

Mrs. Brinkley came in and gave Mekyla a hug. "Hello Mekyla. How's my baby doing?"

"I'm doing okay, mom. How are you holding up?"

"Right now I really don't know. To be honest with you Mekyla, I don't think it has really settled in that I've lost one of my girls. A parent can never imagine one of their children leaving this earth before them. And I think about your father, rest his sole. If this had happened while he was still living, it would definitely have killed him." Mrs. Brinkley wiped a few tears from her face.

Mekyla wrapped her arms around her mom again. "Mom, we're all here for you. You know, either I said it to Christy or she said it to me. But we were just talking about how 'there's no greater love than a mother's love', other than the big man above of course."

"I want a hug," Tere said, as she wrapped her arms around both Mekyla and Mrs. Brinkley.

"So mom," said Mekyla. I see a lot of covered dishes on the kitchen counter. What's all that?"

"Some neighbors brought over some chicken and rolls. But I thought I would cook us something special myself."

"Great, we're on your heels."

"We?" said Tere.

Mekyla turned and rolled her eyes. "Yes we, Tere, do you do anything? Ashton just let you get away with everything. You must have some good –"

"Mekyla don't you even say it. And yes, I must," Tere said as they began to laugh.

Stoney slapped Ashton on the shoulder with the back of his hand. "Ashton, why don't you take me over to this one lady's house?"

"Okay. Who is that, and aren't you married?"

"Oh I can see now, you and Tere are still in the first stages of your marriage."

Termaine laughed. "Unc, I'll take you," he said. "I need to go and pick up my little honey anyway."

Stoney raised his eyebrows. "Wait a minute Termaine, are all of the items on your car legitimate, because I can't afford for us to get pulled over. Because when you picked me up this morning, I distinctly remember us being on the side of an officer at a stop light and it took you have of the green light before we even began to move."

"Unc, I stay clean, moms is an insurance agent. I was just having a flash back of another situation that happened a while back."

"That reminds me, I need to ask Mekyla about some insurance."

Mekyla poked her head back into the living room from the kitchen. "We don't have any that will cover you."

"What? You don't even know what kind I need."

"It doesn't matter Stoney. I don't have any that will cover you, fix you, or even mend you."

Stoney chuckled and shook his head. "That's wrong. Let's go Termaine. I'll just keep my bootleg insurance. You try to make things right and your own family won't help you."

CHAPTER THIRTY-SEVEN
HOW COLD IS IT?

"Hey you, I was just calling to say that I would love to see you after the funeral."

"That's probably not a good idea Jennifer."

"Why do we have to put off what we already have? I want to take care of you."

"It's too soon Jennifer. I shouldn't have done what I done before. If Christy's sisters knew; I would probably lose my kids."

"You're the father, why would you lose your kids? Besides, Mekyla knows remember."

"I'm not going to have this conversation with you Jennifer. It was wrong for me to have sex with you on the same day I lost my wife."

"So you're now going to punish me. You made promises to me Trey and I'm not going to allow you to break it."

"Are you threatening me Jennifer?"

"No, I'm just stating what I feel. And I feel that you owe me the opportunity to have a real relationship with you. I've invested a lot of time in you, and have been faithful to you Trey."

"Just give me a little time to sort everything out. No pressure; right now Jennifer. My children are the most important things in my life right now. They need me more than ever."

"Don't forget Trey, you have a child with me as well."

"That's different Jennifer. And you really don't have to keep bringing that up right now, because that hasn't been confirmed."

"Let's not fight Trey. I just want to be wherever you are. I'm sorry if I seem insensitive to the loss of Christy. I'm not, it's just that I don't want to waste anymore time without you."

"I have another call coming in Jennifer, let's continue this another time."

"I'll be over... Hello, hello." Jennifer said, as she noticed the dial tone on the phone.

"Hello," a very frustrated voice cried out.

"Hello Trey, did I catch you at a bad time?

"Oh, hey Mrs. Brinkley, no of course not, how are you doing?"

"I was just calling to see if you would bring the kids over to have some dinner with us. All of the family is here. And you're welcome to bring your Mr. and Mrs. Love."

"Thank you for the invite. I think I will take you up on that offer. The kids and I for sure will be over there. I'll check with my folks."

"Well, we'll see you soon then. Goodbye. Schonda, make your self useful and stir those greens for me." Mrs. Brinkley said, as she was hanging up the phone.

"Tere, watch the baby for me."

"I got her", Mrs. Brinkley said and she began to multitask. "So, have you and Deon come up with a name yet?"

"I was thinking about naming her Kristian Erin, you know after Christy and also giving her the name Christy suggested."

"That would be just wonderful Schonda, just wonderful." Mrs. Brinkley said, as she stared at Kristian and drifting into deep thought, while slowly rocking the baby back and forward.

"Mama, are all of the arrangements complete?"

"Yes, everything is just about done. Oh, that was Trey on the phone. I invited him and the kids over. After all he's still my son-in-law."

"For now he is," Mekyla said, under her breath. So there's absolutely nothing else that we need to do, to make sure everything goes to plan?"

"Now, I've said no Mekyla. You're welcome to look it over yourself."

"I didn't mean anything by that mom, I just wanted to

make sure that's all."

"Mekyla, what's going on with you? I heard you mumble, what's that all about?" Schonda said, as she pulled Mekyla to the side.

"I just have a lot on my plate right now, you know, losing Christy, who was one of my best friends in addition to my own personal challenges. This is really taking a toll on me."

"We're all feeling it in our own way. But let me know if you need to relieve anything from your mind. You know I'm a good listener."

"Thanks Schonda, I will, but maybe after the funeral okay."

"Not so fast Mekyla. What was the mumbling about?"

"That can wait as well. I promise I will tell you after the funeral."

"Tell her what?" Tere blurted out in a whisper.

"After the funeral Tere, I'll tell you guys after the funeral." Mekyla said, as she began to walk away.

"Schonda, would you see who's at the front door?"

"Yea, okay." Schonda said, as she left the room, still a little puzzled from her previous conversation.

"Stoney, what's up? While reaching to give Stoney a big hug, Schonda asked. When did you get into town?"

"I got in this morning."

"It's really good to see you. How long has it been, it seems like ages. So Termaine has been chauffeuring you around, huh. Hello nephew."

"Hey what's up Auntie Schonda?"

"Will you be bringing Cheyenne over after the funeral Termaine?"

"No, her mother and I are still on, well not so good terms right now. I can barely see her on a good day."

"I thought all of that craziness was over."

"No, I just haven't really said that much about it."

"Well give her a kiss for me, when you see her again. That's just nonsense." Schonda said, as she shook her head from side to side.

"I'll get the door?" Schonda said, as she headed for the door again.

"Well hello Trey. And how are my nieces and nephew doing?"

"Hello Auntie Schonda." The children said, as they one

by one gave Schonda a big hug.

"Come on in guys. Your grandma is around here somewhere with my child, your cousin Kristian."

"Kristian, you named her after Christy?" Trey said, as he looked over at Schonda.

"Yes, it felt right. Besides, I've always loved the name, it sounds soft. How are you and the kids holding up?"

"I'm just taking one day at a time. Schonda, you probably want to leave the door ajar, Ian was pulling up as we were coming in the door."

"Oh, okay. Hello Ian," Schonda said, as she began to give Ian his hug.

"How's it going Schonda? You don't even look like you just had a baby."

"Well thank you Ian. Thank goodness, it was mostly baby weight. Mekyla's around here somewhere."

"Stoney, how's it going man? Long time no see."

"Trey, you look good for an old man."

"Forget you man, I believe you're one up on me, actually a few up on me. Stoney, have you met Ian?"

"So this is Ian. No, I've heard Mekyla speak of him, but I've never had the opportunity to meet him in person until now," Stoney said, as he extended his hand out to Ian.

"It's finally nice to put a face with the person I've heard so many stories about. Some funny as hell man, you have lived the life."

"Come on into the kitchen man and fix you something to drink."

"I'll just take a beer, if you have one."

"I believe there is some in there."

"Ian grab me one." Trey said, as he had a seat on the sofa.

"Have they told you about my latest endeavor, the one about my visit to the doctor to see if I qualified for a crazy check?"

"No, I don't think any of us girls heard that one, well I've never heard about it," Tere said, as she grabbed herself a seat to hear Stoney's story.

"I was still on the bottle back then."

"Back then," Mekyla blurted out, as she opened the bottled beer for Ian.

"Well, more heavily back then. Can I finish my story?"

"Yea, as long as it's clear."

"Like I was saying; before I was interrupted. I was sitting in the waiting area of the doctor's office. This lady was sitting next to me and in my mind, they were all spies. So, I started to flicker my teeth in and out."

"What do you mean flicker them in and out? Does that even match?" Tere said, as she looked into Stoney's mouth.

"You know how when you have some partials put in and they're not the glued ones. You can maneuver them around with your tongue. But since then, I've had them glued, so stop staring into my mouth Tere."

"I was just trying to get a visual. You can continue."

"So after I see this lady look away in discuss, I still wasn't through trying to impress upon her that I was crazy. I took out my switchblade, laid it on the seat beside me, crossed my legs and arms and looked over at her again, while I began to flicker my teeth again. As if, to dare her to touch my switchblade."

"You are so silly. Mekyla said, as they all began to laugh.

"All you girls come in here and help me fix these kids plates," Mrs. Brinkley said, as she peeked out of the kitchen.

"So, that's it, you just laid the switchblade on the chair. I guess you had to have been there huh, Stoney?"

"At some point Tere, things are going to have to stop going right over your head."

"Forget you Stoney, I got it, I was just being sarcastic."

"Ian, how did you know I was here?"

"I called your office and Marie said that you left early and you weren't at the house. So I figured you would be here."

"I know that I haven't been in the best of moods lately, but I'm glad that you came. Well I'ma head in here and help mama out with feeding the kids. Are you hunger?"

"I passed hungry a couple of hours ago."

"I'll fix you a plate when we're done with the kids."

"Thanks baby."

Trey cell phone begins to ring.

"Trey are you going to answer that?"

"Na man, it's just someone from my office calling," Trey said, as he put that call on vibrate.

"So, what kind of business are you in Stoney?" Ashton asked.

"I'm in a little bit of this and a little bit of that. I focused more on law suites here lately. They seem to be paying the bills okay," Stoney said, with a legitimate look on his face, to confirm what he was saying as he began to light his cigarette.

Shouting as she passed through the room, Mrs. Brinkley said, "Don't light that cigarette in my house Stoney." As Trey's cell phone begins to vibrate, he takes it out to see whose calling.

While noticing the name on the face of Trey's phone, Stoney blurts out. "Man you better answer that, I don't think Jennifer wants to wait on the return call."

"Jennifer, is that Jennifer calling you Trey?" Mekyla said, as she was bringing Ian's plate.

"No, this is someone else, a lady in my office."

"If you and that caller need some privacy, you're welcome to step into one of mama's guess rooms."

"Thanks Mekyla, but no thanks. It can wait," Trey said, as he noticed the look of disappointment on Ian's face.

"What's everybody looking so tense for? Trey, is this enough food for you?"

"Yes ma'am, thank you."

"You're welcome. Let me know if you need anything else."

"Mama he's fine." Mekyla said, as she headed for the kitchen.

As Mrs. Brinkley trailed Mekyla, she put her hand on her shoulder to slow her down and said. "There's no need to be rude Mekyla. This isn't like you. I know and you know that Trey is grieving the loss of Christy as well. So want you tell me what's on your mind."

"I'm sorry mom, I overreacted. I should go. I really need to get myself together. Mama, do you know what Christy's last words were to me? She said Mekyla, I don't want to die, come and get me. That's what my sister said to me mama. Those were her last words to me."

"It's not your fault Mekyla, you done everything you possibly could do to find your sister. Who knows what was going on in her mind to make her do what she did to herself? And it's not for us to question his works or be the judge of that," Mrs. Brinkley said, as she and Mekyla began to embrace each other.

"Is everything okay?"

As Mrs. Brinkley opened her eyes to see who was asking, she replied. "Yes everything is fine Ian."

"Mama, I think I'ma head to the house okay."

"Did you get enough to eat?"

"Yes ma'am, and thanks mom," Mekyla said, while giving Mrs. Brinkley a kiss on the cheek.

Waiting in the wings, Ian steps up behind Mekyla and places his hand around her back to escort her back into the living room.

"Hey guys, I'm getting ready to head out. Stoney, it was really good to see you. Maybe after the funeral tomorrow, we can spend some time together."

As Stoney stood up to give Mekyla a big bear hug, he replied. "I would like that very much Mekyla and I'll see you bright and early tomorrow."

"Schonda, Kristian, I like that name very much. Remember to take it easy, you did just have the child."

"Love you Mekyla and I'll see you tomorrow."

"Kimberly and Tere, bye. Love you to." Mekyla said, as she scanned the room to find her favorite fella.

"Love you girl and drive safe."

While slowly walking up behind Mekyla, Termaine whispers softly in his mother's ear. "I'm right here."

"Hey baby. If you can, I would love to see Cheyenne tomorrow, it would bring such peace to my heart to see my grandbaby."

"I'll try mom, I'll really try."

"Well, if it doesn't happen, give her a big kiss for me."

"I always do. Love you mom."

"Take care of yourself and I'll see you tomorrow."

"Ian, peace out man."

"Alright Termaine. Ashton, Deon and Trey, I'll see you guys tomorrow."

"Alright Ian, take care." As they all begin to reply.

"I would like for you girls to watch over Mekyla, she's taking this really hard."

"Mama, I think she knows a little more than we do about why Christy did what she did."

"Well she can't keep it bottled up like that Schonda, we really need to keep an eye on her. Do you suppose she's blaming Trey for Christy's death? If so, she shouldn't, because I'm sure he had nothing to do with her death. He loved Christy very much."

As Tere began to put the dishes in the dishwasher, she replied. "I don't know, I kinda think there's more to it than we know, concerning Trey's involvement."

"I think so to. You know the way he didn't show up in the beginning when she was first admitted. And Tere, didn't you discover Christy and not Trey?"

"Let's just calm down, he is in the next room. We'll talk about this some more after the funeral. It will probably be good for us to get all of our unanswered questions answered and then put it behind us." Mrs. Brinkley said, as she sat down at the kitchen table.

CHAPTER THIRTY-EIGHT
I'M HIS, UNTIL I'M NOT

"Ian, I'ma stop by my office to check for messages or e-mail that I may have. If anyone calls for me, please just take a message," Mekyla said, as she shouted across the room. "Oh, you scared me Ian." Mekyla said, as she continued to sit down at her desk. "Did you hear me?"

"Yes I heard you."

"Well give me a minute okay?"

"That's all I've been giving you, is a minute. Give me a minute. I need you Mekyla, I need you right now." Ian said, as he kneeled down on his knees and pulled Mekyla close to him.

"What are you doing Ian?"

"I'm getting ready to make love to my woman."

"Please don't Ian."

As Ian placed his index finger up to Mekyla's mouth and then proceeded to raise her skirt above her hips, he began to squeeze the cheeks of her firm butt very hard.

"Ian, sweetie stop."

Ignoring Mekyla's soft rejections, Ian proceeded to take off her panties and then pulling her out of the chair and onto the floor. Where he began to kiss all over her body with soft slow pecks, with only partially removing his pants, Ian began to make passionate love to Mekyla. With small movements of consent, Mekyla began to cry, squeeze and rub Ian's back. Tugging in an effort to remove the rest of his clothes, as Ian raises up to remove his shirt, he grabs Mekyla's hand and takes her to the room where they began to explore one another's bodies in a way that hadn't been explored in a long time. Between moments of pleasure, Ian occasionally whispers in Mekyla's ear. "This feels so good baby, I needed you so bad. I don't ever want to lose you again."

With a look of, what am I doing? Mekyla began to try and apply closure to the moment. "Ian, will you raise up?"

"I'm almost there baby, hold on for one more minute."

"Ian, please get up."

Unable to stop the moment, Ian whispered in Mekyla's ear, "Baby, please don't stop me now."

Sinking more into a moment of total confusion, Mekyla blurts out, "Ian, please roll over."

"Okay baby, hold on." Ian said, as he turned over in an attempt to make himself comfortable in the bed. "Good night Mekyla."

As Mekyla turned to lie on her side, she folded her right arm up under her head and began to cry silent tears.

CHAPTER THIRTY-NINE
I'VE ALWAYS REGRET EATING THE SNICKERS AFTER IT'S GONE

"Good morning."

"Good morning," Mekyla said as she opened her eyes remembering that she was still lying next to Ian.

"This feels good, waking up next to you again. I know I probably rushed it last night, but I needed to hold you baby."

"This was a mistake Ian. I wasn't ready for this."

"You're saying that as if it was dirty what we did. Not to long ago Mekyla, we use to enjoy each other."

"I don't know what's wrong with me Ian. We're burying my sister today." As Mekyla looked into Ian's eyes, she said. "This was too soon for me Ian."

Recognizing the look she had on her face, in an attempt to stop what she was about to say, Ian blurted out, "Don't say it Mekyla."

"Maybe we should try separating, because this ain't working. I don't believe I'm happy anymore. After we bury Christy, I'm going to leave the city for a while. It's time for me to start promoting my book anyway. Should we take separate cars to mom's house?"

"Don't be silly Mekyla, you know that I insist on driving you to your mom's house. Mekyla my heart is in this all the way. If I every lose you, it will tear me apart. Do you hear me? It's going to tear me apart."

As she rose from the bed, Mekyla looked back at Ian and said, "Ian I really need to get in the shower; so that we won't be late for the funeral."

"I know you're not that cold Mekyla. Is this all that I get, after all these years? You're acting as if your words are the only ones that count."

"I asked you to give me time. And you constantly invade my space. Don't you understand that I'm confused as to what I want right now? You're not listening to me. I feel like I've repeated this a hundred times Ian."

While slowly closing the door to the bathroom, Mekyla blurts out. "Just let me go, okay. I'm not good for you, you deserve better."

"Mekyla, I love you. I love you Mekyla. I don't want anybody else. You cheated on me. I've always been faithful to you. Talk to me Mekyla, tell me what I can do different to make this work. Just tell me, I will change." Ian said, as he leaned his head up against the bathroom's door looking downward as he watched some of the tears fall to the floor.

As the water from the shower washed Mekyla's tears away, she took a long pause as she looked over at the bathroom's door, through the glass of the shower.

CHAPTER FORTY
THE MORNING AFTER

"Stoney; wake up. It's time to get up. Termaine, get up son."

"Hey grandma."

"Good morning." "Would you like some breakfast?"

"Yes ma'am."

"Stoney, you want some coffee?"

"Yes, black, with a couple tablespoons of sugar,

please."

CHAPTER FORTY-ONE
LOVE ME LOVE ME NOT

"I'm sorry Ian. I never thought myself to be that insensitive, but those are my feelings. I don't know what other words to use, without someone getting their feelings hurt."

"You know where I stand on this. And I don't know what other words I can use to describe to you how much this is hurting me. Some say that love is complicated, some say love wants too much. But when you know that you've found that special someone; too much is never enough. Mekyla, I wish you the best in whatever it is you're looking for," Ian said, as he headed for the shower.

While holding her towel, Mekyla lowers her head and turns to the closet, grabs a hold of the doorknobs with a slight pause before opening the doors.

Leaning his head back out the door of the bathroom, Ian asks. "Tell me Mekyla, are you going to Austin to be with him?"

"That's not my intentions Ian. I'll probably head for Atlanta, Georgia and a few other places to market my book and then back home to finalize what I'm going to do with my agency."

"Well I guess that it and that's all." Ian said as he returned to the shower.

CHAPTER FORTY-TWO
IT HAS DEFINITELY FROZE OVER

"Hello Trey, this is Jennifer."

"Jennifer, how did you get the house number?"

"I called my cell phone from your house the other night, so that I could lock it in."

"What's up Jennifer, you know I'm getting ready for my wife's funeral."

"Yes, that's why I was calling. I wanted to be there as well. Do you think the family would mind?"

"Why do you need to be there?"

"I would like to pay my respects."

"Well okay, if it's just to pay your respects, why would the family have a problem with that?"

"I don't know, maybe because we're sleeping together."

"The family doesn't know that. Only Mekyla and I would like to keep it that way. And I really don't think she knows that we were sleeping together."

"And you're talking for how long Trey?"

"For as long as it takes. Don't get cocky on me Jennifer, I'm burying my wife today and our kids are going to be there."

"I'm not just anyone Trey, I'm also a mother of your child."

"Let's not go there okay. That hasn't been verified. I need to go Jennifer." Trey said, as he hung up the phone.

As Jennifer took a pause to look at her cell phone, she said, "I know he didn't just hang up in my face. I'm not going to be disrespected."

CHAPTER FORTY-THREE
LEFT TOO SOON

"Termaine did you bring your clothes over here?"

"Yes ma'am. They're out in the car. Good morning unc."

"Morning, Termaine. Hey Auntie, did mama leave or is she still here?" Stoney asked.

"No, she went on to the house."

"My intentions were to leave with her."

"Those may have been your intentions Stoney, but there was no way you were getting in your mama's car, as intoxicated as you were last night."

"I was feeling pretty good."

"Yes you were, yes you were Stoney. I can't believe I'm burying one of my daughters this afternoon. Mm, mm, mm, she hadn't even begun to really live her life. Lord please give me the strength to get through this day." Mrs. Brinkley said, while shaking her head side to side as she headed for her bedroom.

"Hey unc, I'll be back, I need to run an errand."

"Alright Termaine, see you in a bit man."

CHAPTER FORTY-FOUR
CLOSURE IN ITS FINAL STAGES

"Ian, I'm heading for mama's house. Were you going to meet me there or at the church?"

"No, I'm going to take you there, like I said earlier. There's no need to drive two cars."

"When this is all over, I'll come back and pack my things, okay."

"Whatever you feel you need to do Mekyla. Just know that there's no rush for you to remove you or your things."

While holding her hand on the front door doorknob, Mekyla turned to Ian to say. "I know Ian. It's just that I probably shouldn't put it off any longer. I don't want it to get to a point where we can't even speak anymore. "And by the way, I got my period."

With a look of disappointment Ian replied, "Okay, okay."

CHAPTER FORTY-FIVE
DON'T BE TOO LATE AGAIN

"Stoney would you get the door." Mrs. Brinkley said, at the sound the doorbell chiming.

"Hey what's going on Stoney? Aren't we looking mighty handsome?"

"Thank you Tere. Hey what's up Ashton?"

"Not too much man, not too much. You had a nice time last night." Ashton said, as he headed for the kitchen.

"Man, half that stuff I don't even remember. Ashton, pour me another cup of coffee." Stoney said, as he leaned his hand out with cup in hand.

"Good morning mama Brinkley." Ashton said, while giving her a big bear hug.

"Good morning sweetie, don't you look awful handsome."

"Thank you, mama Brinkley."

"Tere, you look beautiful as always."

"Thank you mom, so do you." Tere said, as a few teardrops began to swell up in her eyes.

"Here you go sweetie, you'll probably want to take this towel with you to the funeral."

"You're probably right mama, I don't want to find myself with a bunch of little tissue remnants on my face. I've seen it happen before and it wasn't a pretty sight." Tere said as she laughed and cried at the same time.

"Stoney..."

"I know auntie, get the door. Hey what's going on Schonda, Deon and family? Come on in." Stoney said, as he held the door for everyone to come in.

In a moment of remembrance and passing through to give her arriving guest their hugs, Mrs. Brinkley blurted out, "Stoney call your mom to see if she's on her way."

"Everyone look so nice. Schonda bring my newest granddaughter over here so that I can give her one of those big sloppy grandma kisses."

While making funny faces at her grandchild, Mrs. Brinkley jumped a little startled by the doorbell.

"Would someone get that door please?"

"Mom, it's the limousine drivers. Come on in please." Kimberly said, while escorting the two men into the house.

"I guess this is it guys. We're burying Christy today we're burying my baby today. Is everyone here, if so, let's go ahead and load up in the cars?"

"Mama, Trey and the kids haven't gotten here yet." As she made her way over to Mrs. Brinkley, Tere cried out. "And where is Kimberly?"

"I thought I saw Kimberly in the back room."

"Oh and Trey's pulling up in the drive now, but what about Mekyla?"

"Oh yea, my baby, has anyone heard from Mekyla?"

"Grandma, I just talked to mom and she should be pulling up in a couple of minutes."

"Thanks baby."

"Grandma, how much longer are you going to call me baby, I'm a grown man now?"

"I will call you baby, stinka, or whatever else I want to call you, for as long as I got breath in my body. Is that Mekyla pulling up?"

"Yes ma'am. I'll go out and get her."

"Okay, good Schonda, then I guess we're now ready to go."

With a slight adjustment to her hat, Mrs. Brinkley made her way to the limousine.

"Mom I have something to tell you."

"Hey baby, what is it?"

"What I was trying to tell you on the phone was that I ran into Cheyenne's mom and her new boyfriend that got all up in my face."

"Okay, I don't really like the sound in your voice. And?"

"Well, we had words and he threatened to put his boys on me if I ever came around my daughter while he's there."

"What, now that doesn't make any since Termaine. Please tell me you just walked away from that madness."

"Well, no I didn't. What had happened was..." Interrupted by a voice coming from the limousine, Mekyla turned to say, "I'm coming. Termaine were going to have to talk about this later okay?"

"Yea, okay."

CHAPTER FORTY-SIX
MAY YOU ALWAYS WATCH OVER HER

As the minister began to wrap up the personal goodbyes from family and friends, Mekyla began making her way to the podium to say her goodbyes to Christy, as she passed by her mom she gave a soft rub across the shoulder.

"Hello everyone, I would like to thank you for coming today to say goodbye to my sister Christy. The only way I felt I could express myself, is through a poem. So if you would bid me this moment to read this poem I would appreciate it."

"Go ahead baby." A voice cried out from one of the pews.

"My poem to Christy is entitled 'When my tears cry.'" Mekyla said, as she unfolded the paper she had clutched to her side.

"When the day is over, memories are made. When the morning comes forsake us, we become sad and maybe a little blue. My how time passes when I... I'm sorry this is not the one I chose to read today. Please give me a moment." Mekyla said, as she fumbled through the papers.

"Okay here we go."

The poem
"When my Tears Cry"

Was there something I could have done, was there something I could have said to take your mind off the horrible thought of wishing you were dead. What hurt you so bad to bring you to this, did you think about your family and how you'd be missed?

Until we meet again I must say goodbye, but in the back of my mind I will always wonder why.

I am so angry with you for not coming to me, to talk out your problems, how bad could they be?

I would have held you in my arms, on my shoulder, our heads would lay with forgiving humble hearts to God we would pray.

Dear God, give us strength and keep us sane, to deal with the things that we cannot change. Bless our lives with happiness and love, as given from our father in the heavens above.

Bless those who brought pain to us and hurt our loving hearts and me and you as sisters shall never depart. Amen.

As Mekyla closed her eyes and took a deep breath, she concluded.

Until we meet again, I release you with love to watch over me day and night from the heavens above.

As the room filled with tears and silence, Mekyla rubbed her hand against the casket in which Christy lie still in and paused for a brief moment.

"This isn't fair." Words mumbled in a whisper as Mekyla made her way back to her seat.

"That was a very beautiful poem Mekyla."

"Thank you, mama." Mekyla said putting her hands around her mother to console her as the minister began to say the closing prayer before moving Christy's body to the atrium. As they all began to line up single file to view the body, the room again filled with tears and moans.

"Mekyla."

"Yes. Oh, hello Jennifer, thank you for coming."

"I'm really sorry about this, I'm truly sorry about this." Jennifer said, as she jumped in line behind Mekyla to become nearer to Trey.

"Hello Jennifer."

"Hello Trey." Jennifer said, raising her eyebrow with a smirk on her face.

Moving closer to Jennifer's ear, Trey remarked in a very low voice, "Well I see you made your way into the family section."

"I've always been like family; I guess you can say, even more so now." Jennifer said in a smart voice, as she looked over her shoulder at Trey while saying her goodbyes to Christy.

"Jennifer."

"Oh, Mrs. Brinkley, I'm sorry but you scared me."

"My mother always told me that, "If you jump all the time, you must be doing something you're not supposed to be doing," now what is it that's making you jump like that here at my daughter's funeral?"

"I guess just being at another funeral again so soon. You know I just buried my grandmother?" In an attempt to divert the conversion, because she wasn't sure how much if any that Mrs. Brinkley saw between her and Trey.

"Oh yes, you did. I'm really sorry to hear about your loss as well. Now why don't you run along up there and be with Mekyla, okay."

"Sure, Mrs. Brinkley, of course I should be with Mekyla for support. And how are you holding up by the way?"

"I don't believe it will ever be easy to bury one of your children, so to answer your question, I don't really know right now Jennifer." Mrs. Brinkley said, as she began to make her way to the limousine awaiting her.

Not feeling comfortable enough anymore, Jennifer made her way to her own car to attend the burial at the cemetery.

CHAPTER FORTY-SEVEN
WHAT HAPPENS NEXT

"Have all the kids received plates?" Tere said, as she cried out across the room.

"I believe so Tere, if they're hungry they will find their way into the kitchen. How are you holding up sweetie, are you okay?"

"I don't know Mekyla, I really don't know." Tere answered, slipping into a silent breakdown while sliding down the wall of the kitchen in tears with her hands up against her forehead.

Kneeling to the floor with Tere, Mekyla began to cry as she began to comfort her little sister.

"We're going to get through this you hear me, we're going to get through this, all of us together."

"Are you guys okay? Can I help or get you anything?"

"Thanks Ashton, but I think we're just going to sit here on the floor and cry until we just can't cry anymore. As a matter of fact, you can do something for us. Please make us both a very stiff drink...how about that. Actually another thing is can someone get Tere some type of towel or wet napkin so that she can clean this mascara that has smeared all over her face." Mekyla said, as she began to remove her shoes in an attempt to make herself comfortable on the kitchen floor.

"How bad is it Mekyla?"

"It's pretty bad. So bad, I didn't know whether to laugh or cry a few minutes ago."

"You're wrong for that Mekyla." Tere said, as they both began to laugh and shake their heads.

"Mom, are you doing okay wherever you are?" Mekyla said, as she hollered to the other rooms.

"Why are you sitting on the floor? I'm not sitting on the floor with you guys."

"Didn't anybody ask you to Kimberly, but since you brought it up and pretending you're too good for the floor, plant her right here beside me." Tere said, as she pulled at Kimberly's hand.

"Can we at least sit at the table? I'm sure this floor is dirty and I'm in a very nice dress." Still hesitating to sit on the floor, Kimberly remarked.

"Who's saying my floor is dirty?" Mrs. Brinkley shouted.

"Kimberly." Tere and Mekyla said simultaneously.

"Okay, ya'll know that wasn't necessary to repeat."

"Here you go ladies, Kimberly would you like a drink?"

"Yes, thank you Ashton. What are we having anyway, Shirley Temples, because you know I don't really drink and they neither do they."

"You are today. We're going to get drunk in our mother's house. Mom does it all the time."

"Shut up Mekyla, mama doesn't know we know that." Kimberly said, in a soft whisper. "And the term is, "She's feeling lifted."

"Yes she does, she just doesn't care anymore. You

must have forgotten about the, 'I'm grown' speech she use to give us all the time."

"No Tere, I remember the speech vaguely, but I thought she stopped."

"She stopped. Stopped saying I'm grown." Mekyla said, as they all began to laugh.

"I wanta join you girls." Schonda said, as she began to pull up a chair.

"Grab yourself a glass of orange juice or something and scoot in close to us." Mekyla said, as she propped her feet up onto Schonda's chair.

"The girls are having some kind of powwow in there. Mrs. Brinkley, the guys and I are going to head for your den and watch some sports, if that's okay."

"No, I don't mind at all Deon. You guys know where everything is, just make yourself at home. So Stoney, are you leaving out today or tomorrow?"

"My flight leaves in the morning around ten. Hey auntie, I'ma go back here with the fellas, you and mom can hang out and do whatever it is you do now." Stoney said, as he began to head towards the den.

"Well, I guess we're too old for him to hang around. Jean, are you getting sleepy?"

"Girl yes, I was still sleepy when I woke up this morning. My bones just can't handle all this moving around briskly anymore."

"I don't know about you, but I'ma head to my room and stretch out across the bed for a bit. It's plenty of room, if you wanta come."

"I'm right behind you."

"Girls, me and your auntie are going to go stretch out across the bed for a little bit, keep an eye on your kids okay. And if any of my girlfriends stop by, thank them and let them know that I will get back with them soon."

"Alright mama, see you when you wake up Auntie Jean." Schonda said, as they resumed the conversation they were having.

Before the doorbell could finish its first chime, Stoney yelled out, I got it. "Hmm and who do we have here?"

"Stoney, it's me Jennifer. Now don't tell me you don't remember me. Jennifer, I'm Mekyla's buddy."

"Well time has been very good to you." Stoney said, as

he looked Jennifer up and down.

"Thanks Stoney. Where is Mekyla?"

"All the girls are in the kitchen go right on in there with your fine self."

"Yea." Jennifer said, as she shook her head with a smile of whatever on her face.

"Jennifer, hey girl, come on in and find a seat." Kimberly said, as she stood to give Jennifer a hug.

"Hello everyone, it was okay for me to stop by right?"

As Mekyla raised her eyebrow, she said. "Girl you have never said that since I've known you, what's up?"

"Nothing, I just didn't want to intrude."

"Only strangers intrude, you're like family right.

"Girl, come on in and have a seat and stop talking non-sense." Kimberly said.

"What are you guys drinking? Whatever you're having, I'll take a double."

"I got you Jennifer." Tere said, as she began to fix Jennifer's drink.

"So Jennifer, Mekyla tells us you went to Louisiana." Tere said, as she put together what thought to be her masterpiece drink for Jennifer.

Kinda looking away to avoid eye contact with Mekyla, Jennifer replied, "Oh, yes, I did. It was nothing though."

"Oh yea, your trip, Jennifer want you tell us about your trip and don't say it was nothing, because you were very exited the last time we talked. Something about Brent somebody, that's the second time I've forgotten his name." Mekyla said, as she gestured for another refill.

"Oh, it's nothing."

"Will you stop saying it's nothing and tell the damn story." Kimberly said, as she made her way to islander to make herself another drink.

"Kimberly," Schonda said, as she began to apologize to Jennifer on Kimberly's behalf, saying that it was the liquor speaking.

"Well they keep going back and forward like it's a big secret or something. Jennifer, Mekyla's going to tell us the story, so tell us the story."

"It's okay Schonda, Kimberly's right, I'll tell the story." Drinking more than half of the drink that was made for her, Jennifer began to say, "Okay well Mekyla, you remember me

111

saying how I went by the Ms Cashmere's shop there in Louisiana?"

"Oh yes, and something about her brother. But kind of re-cap, because I don't quite remember."

"Well, when I got back from Louisiana, I met up with who I thought was her brother, Brent Elliott, who is now here in Tulsa coaching a football team. To later discover that he's her husband."

"Then who was the guy with her that night at the game?"

"That gorgeous hunk of a man was her brother."

"Was he at the shop that day as well?"

"No I didn't see him."

"That's too bad, huh?" Mekyla said, as she raised her glass in the air. "He was fine y'all."

"Mekyla, Ian's in the other room." Tere said, in a very low voice.

"Ian and I are on a break, because I'm screwed up."

"Mekyla, we're going to deal with that later. So, who are these people you guys are talking about?"

"I'll tell you later, along with my crap. Go ahead and finish the story Jennifer."

"I get home and meet up with Brent Elliott, only to discover that he's really not my son's father."

"Hold up. Son, what son are you talking about? When did you have a son Jennifer?"

"Almost eighteen years ago Kimberly. His name is, well we call him Junior. I named him Brent Elliott, after who I thought, was his father."

"Man, that's kind of messed up, huh? Is it just me, or didn't we think Junior was her brother?" Tere said, as she scanned the room for feedback.

"Yes Tere, you're right. I did tell everyone he was my brother, because of personal reasons."

"So Jennifer, was there an alternate, a possible or something?"

"Yes, actually there is and Brent is the one who actually brought it to my attention, when he denied the possibility of being my son's father."

"Dang, was it like that?" Kimberly said, as she made her way back over to a spot on the floor.

"I guess I was so caught up in knowing that it was

definitely him, that I didn't even look to any other options."

In a very curious voice Mekyla says. "And who was the alternate Jennifer?"

"Mekyla, I would really rather not say right now."

"Why, it's not like any of us probably knows him, right? Just tell us Jennifer."

"I would really rather not guys."

"There you go again and you want to be apart of our sisterhood. You're not winning any brownie points with me for sure."

"Kimberly it's just that I don't know how you guys are going to respond to this. Let me just preference it with, bare in mind that this happened over eighteen years ago, way before I knew any of you really, other than Mekyla."

Based upon that last comment, Mekyla began to shift all of her attention to the answer Jennifer was about to give.

"The father of Junior is Trey."

"Trey! Trey who, our Trey? My sister's Trey?"

"Hey what's up, did someone call me?"

"Trey."

"Yea, it's me in the flesh what's up."

"No, we're not calling you. We're just responding to what Jennifer said."

"What Jennifer said?" Looking over at Jennifer with a face of confusion, Trey asks.

"So what did Jennifer say to have you calling out my name so many times?"

"She said...."

"Tere, what are you about to say?" Schonda blurted out.

"Well Jennifer put it on the table, I'm just addressing it."

"Instead of us all sitting here looking like we don't know what to say next, we might as well get it over with. So again, I'm going to attempt to say. Jennifer said that you are the father of her son. Now there you have it, I said it, now what? No, actually I'm not through."

"Okay here we go, Tere in mama's house, is really not the place right now, please."

"Schonda, we're all grown here and mama is going to know before all of our feet leave her house, trust. So like I was going to say, this little information that we're now being made aware of, would this be the problem that caused my sister to commit suicide?"

With the room still filled with much confusion, Mekyla looked to Jennifer or Trey to answer the question.

"Come on ladies, I just buried my wife, your sister."

"Trey, this is not the time to get all politically correct on us. Just answer the damn question and we can move on."

"Well Tere, it's not that simple. So, I'm going to have to say yes and no."

"I'm going to need for you to be very specific in your attempt to answer that same question Trey."

"Before I even knew about this kid, Christy found out that Jennifer and I were having an affair. She didn't know about the kid at all, only the affair."

Standing to her feet, Mekyla reaches over and grabs Jennifer's face and gives her a big kiss and says, "Jennifer, I was somewhat there with you on the child issue because it was so long ago and before my sister and because I know all the other details as to what you went through these last eighteen years of you life. But now that you've stepped into the present with this bull of having an affair with my brother-in, ex brother-in-law, you're going to have to step. And I don't ever want to see your conniving face again."

Looking over at Trey, Jennifer says. "Trey, are you coming?"

"Jennifer, you need to be worrying about you getting out the door, right about now."

"Trey, if you weren't the father of our niece and nephews, trust, we will be beating you down right now. So, you need to gather your things and leave also."

"I don't want any trouble either. So, I'm going to get my kids and we're leaving."

"If I thought I had a chance of getting custody of those children, I would definitely go for it."

"Kimberly, the only way you're going to get my children, is over my dead body."

"Whatever it takes Trey, whatever it takes."

"Okay, this is getting out of hand, Trey would you just go ahead and leave please." Schonda said, as she did for all situations that needed mediation.

"You know what everyone; I now know I need time away from Tulsa. I'm going to head out to promote my book in a couple of days."

"I wish I had something to promote, so that I can run away from my problems to."

"I'm not running away from my problems, this really isn't my problem Tere."

"Yes you are, you have a man in there that loves you to pieces and you don't even know how to show him love back."

"That's why he deserves someone better than me."

"You're going to regret those words one day Mekyla. But I truly hope not, because I believe you are sincere in your inability to love, it just takes patience and determination."

"I truly love my family's concern, but it's time for me to take a chance on me."

"We love you too Mekyla. I'm going in there and get my baby's daddy and head home."

"I'm right behind you Schonda. Ashton should be ready to go as well, it's been a long day, a very long day."

"I guess I'll go in there and hug my mama and my aunt, because as you can see, I don't have a man in there waiting to take me home."

"Take Ian, Mekyla doesn't want him."

"Can I Mekyla?"

"Kimberly, you and Tere better go' on with that. Just because I don't want him right now, still doesn't change the selfish fact of not wanting to share him with no one else. So, if you ladies don't mind, I'm going in there to get the man that I'm on a break with."

"Mekyla, Ian left a little while ago."

"Get out. He didn't even say goodbye? Forget him then. Okay Kimberly, I'll hold you, if you take me to Ian's house to, I guess pack my stuff, huh."

"Girl, your stuff will probably be packed when you get there." Tere said, as they all began to laugh.

"When I come down off this liquor high, this really isn't going to be that funny. But it is now. Another thing guys, mama really doesn't have to know all of this right now, we did just bury her daughter. Let's just let her get over this for a while, okay?"

"I'm with you on that one Mekyla." Schonda said, as she stood in the doorway of the kitchen.

"Me too."

"Thanks Kimberly, see ya Schonda. What about you Tere?"

"Okay, only if you let me have some of my people do a back alley on Jennifer."

"What people, you don't have any people. Just go with us on this for a while and we'll take care of the Jennifer, Trey thing later. Is that a deal?"

"Deal." Everyone said in unison.

CHAPTER FORTY-EIGHT
HIS SILENT CRIES

"Son, I'm glad you showed up here at your grandma's house."

"Moms are you okay?"

"Yes, over time I'm going to be just fine. I'm also glad you showed up because I wanted to tell you in person that I will be going away for a little while to promote my book."

"I knew that was going to happen, but I guess I didn't know it was going to happen this soon. Okay, did you need me to be on the road with you?"

"No, not at first, but I will send for you when the sales get out of hand," looking over at Termaine with this big grin on her face, she replied to her own statement. "Yea, I can hardly wait for that to happen."

"Oh yea mom, it's going to happen, it's going to happen and I'm going to be your number one fan."

"Thanks baby, that's sweet."

"Hey mom, is it okay if I just drop you off? Oh girl is waiting for me to stop by and pick her up."

"Oh girl huh, I'm sure her parents gave her a name, but I'm also sure you saying 'oh girl' for all of them, keeps you safe, right?"

"Something like that."

"What, did Ian pre-plan this with you or something? You know what; I didn't mean to ask you that. Everything is okay, Kimberly is going to take me to the house. Love ya and I'll keep in touch. Oh, did you want to tell me what it was that was on your mind? You had mentioned something earlier about Cheyenne's mom."

"Oh, I took care of that, but we'll talk later. Love you mom, have a safe journey and I'll kiss that grandchild of yours for you, I'm sure things are getting ready to change into my favor."

"Thanks baby and I don't know if I like the tone of what you just said, about you handling it. But like you said, we'll talk later when we have time. Bye."

Final Chapter Three months later

CHAPTER SIXTY-FIVE
THE BOOK SIGNING

As Mekyla was signing her books, she pulled the next one to her without looking up and saying 'your name please'. Then a deep voice called out.

"JB."

"JB. So, JB, what would you like for me to say in your book?"

"You can write to JB, my number one fan."

As Mekyla began to write, she said, "I'm sorry, but my son already has that spot. Here you go sir." Mekyla said, while raising her head to offer her signed book. "Jonathan."

"I thought it ended all wrong."

"What do you mean?"

"I felt like Lisa walked away with no closure and no love in her life."

"Lisa was married."

"But Lisa found something better than marriage."

"Please share with us on what Lisa found outside of her marriage."

"I believe Lisa for the very first time, allowed her self to fall in love. And it scared her so bad that she ran away. She's a runner. And I'm here to let the author no that I have the answer to her situation."

A person from the line cried out. "I got that same feeling."

"Okay." Mekyla said, as she began to smile of embarrassment. "So how are you going to rewrite an ending that's already published?"

"By starting a new beginning and by telling her that I won't begin to make a lot of promises that all women want to hear. But that I will give it my best each and every day."

Standing up from her seat, Mekyla whispered, "I'm gonna have to really finish signing these books."

"I understand, but first I would like to give you this ticket to Austin and I don't want to get dramatic in front of your crowd here. But, here's also a ring, asking for your hand in marriage." As Mekyla looked at the ring in aw, she sat back in her chair speechless.

"I'll be waiting Mekyla; I'll be waiting as long as I have to. I lost you once, it's not going to happen again."

As Jonathan walked away, the lady next in line blurted out. "Ms. Williams, you better run after that man, I mean run okay."

"Thank you for that. And what is your name darling and what would you like for me to write?"

BACK AT THE HOTEL

"Oh it's so nice to be able to lie down and sleep. Who's this calling me, I'm so tired." Mekyla said, as she reached for her cell phone.

"Hello."

"Hello Mekyla, its Ian. I was just calling to make sure you were still coming home tomorrow."

"Home tomorrow, wow these three months has gone by pretty fast huh? Yes, I'm looking at a ticket that says I'm going to be in Tulsa tomorrow Ian."

"I'll be there to pick you up Mekyla. Mekyla?"

"Yes Ian."

"I love you. I still love you."

"Baby steps Ian. Let's just see how it's going to go tomorrow okay?"

"Okay. It's going to be good to see you. It's been a long time."

"Goodnight Ian."

"Goodnight Mekyla."

HOUSTON INTERNATIONAL AIRPORT

As Mekyla scrounged around for her ticket, her hand bumped the little box. She heard the announcement. Now boarding flight 881 for Tulsa International Airport, we're now boarding flight 881 for Tulsa International Airport.

"What am I doing? I have to get on this plane, I can't be doing something I'm not sure of again. I need to focus and get on the plane." Mekyla said, as she began to trot to the boarding area.

"Would it be okay for me to bring my own bag of Lay's Chips on this flight?"

"Yes ma'am, that's not a problem. Enjoy your flight." The attendant said as he open the rope for Mekyla to board. Digging in her purse to grab her cell phone now with only twenty minutes before landing, Mekyla makes a phone call.

"Hello."

"Hello, this is Mekyla, you're going to be there to pick me up right?"

"Yes I'm going to be there."

"I caught a different flight I'll be there in twenty minutes. I'm coming in on Southwest Airlines."

"I'll be there."

"Okay, see you when I land."

Rounding the isle and looking down the way of the boarding area, Mekyla begins to trot. And as she became closer, she dropped all of her luggage in hand and threw her hands in the air, in anticipation to hold him. "I don't ever want to lose you again." She whispers in his ear, so tell me, do you have some very large strawberries with whip cream and a little sprinkle of sugar at the house waiting on me?

"On the nightstand in a bowl you will not only find those big plump, freshly picked and each one having been tasted by me there, but as well a bottle of the finest wine very chilled next to it."

"I would have you take advantage of me any other way." Mekyla said, as she began to kiss the man of her dreams.

THE END
**Or,
Is it?**

This story will continue with
"Tears of Katrina"
&
Termaine's story will continue with
"Judging Cheyenne's Shadow"

Both to be released sometime in 2006'
I hope you enjoyed the read.

Be sure to visit my website **www.vanessahollis.com** or
www.teardropspublishing.com

To verify the latest mailing addresses…thanks

Book Club Notes & Questions:

_____

_____

_____

_____

_____

_____

_____

_____

_____

_____

_____

_____

_____

_____

_____

_____

_____

_____

_____

_____

_____

_____

_____

_____